PROPOSAL FOR AN EMPATHETIC SURVEILLANCE STATE

Rene Franco

Published by Paper Plane Pilot Publishing
Los Angeles, California
www.thepaperplanepilots.com

Cover design by *Laura Khayat*
Interior art by *Rene Franco*
Interior design by *Sara Khayat*
Edited by *Sara Khayat & Michael J. Hetzler*
Proofread by *Michael J. Hetzler & Sara Khayat*

ISBN-13: *978-0-9979836-2-3*
ISBN-10: *0-9979836-2-0*

This copy is a first edition.

THE MUSE COMPLEX

You meet online. Because of course you do. Her first lie sits right next to her name: her age. She confesses, stuck at the top of the Ferris wheel at the Santa Monica Pier. You've just asked her for exclusivity rights. The negotiation is taking much longer than you presumed it would.

But that's later. Right now she's just moved here. She escaped a backwards-ass town from Georgia, close to Atlanta, but not close enough. So she's here for something having to do with fashion journalism at FIDM. She isn't working yet because she's going to class full-time.

In 3 months, when you ask her about her color theory assignment, she'll blow smoke in your face from the $250 glass bong you bought her as she tells you she's stopped going to class.

But right now, she's excited to meet you. She wants to hear everything you have to say about living up in the Bay. She wants to see your photography, which you make sure to mention almost immediately when she asks you about hobbies. She's excited to smoke with you while listening to Childish Gambino. But mostly she keeps saying how much she *fucking wants you*.

All your plans to meet up and actualize this Instagram-meme-of-a-romance keep falling through. She goes back to Georgia for a while. She comes back, moves out of the valley to the Westside, closer to you. You tell her you're dying to take her to one of the loft parties at the new property your company just bought along the Venice Boardwalk. She says she forgot her contacts back in Georgia and doesn't want to meet you wearing glasses in spite of your protests that you think nerds are sexier than basic girls. She leaves L.A. again. She stops texting you with that urgency that makes you know you're almost always on her mind.

By the time you finally do meet, she's gone all Woodward and Bernstein on your brown ass. She's dug up all the key plot points you've allowed to be public. There's a video she tracks down—a mini viral sensation you made for work as a joke. You play this weirdo hipster who never gets laid because he's consumed too many Woody Allen and John Cusack films and can't quite get it together to actually ever approach a girl. He just spends time talking about all the things he would do. The magical day trip he'd take his chosen girl on. The lame poems and songs he'd compose in her name. The face he'd make while he was "really listening."

This whole thing is supposed to be ridiculous and hilarious as it becomes apparent he's not looking for a girl who actually resembles these sincere qualities, but one who is appropriating and cutting out components of the personalities of various manic pixie dream girls (e.g. Natalie Portman in *Garden State*, Kate Hudson in *Almost Famous*, Zooey Deschanel in everything).

It's very ironic.

You've walked all the way to the pier and there are twirling lights forming pink and yellow smiles the first time you kiss her.

She's melting. She thinks your not being white is sexy. She asks if you actually wear glasses like you did in the video. You tell her you don't; her head slinks down with a tinge of disappointment.

She keeps asking you about your job and tells you that she is (obviously) an avid user of your app. You tell her you see yourself as a creative: the equivalent of a Matisse or a Jeff Koons but for the twenty-something crowd. You give people the ability to transform the mundane into art. She says she never saw it that way but she always thought the body belonging to the brain who came up with vomiting rainbows must be "really fit and hot."

You tell her that was you.

She mentions that in her travels of stalking you she found some of your photography. There's a series you presented at the Coulter Gallery in Stanford for your senior thesis show. They were glossy, gelatin black and white prints of scans from the photo books of famous war photographers. It was not well received. She loved them and couldn't get over how "pretty and shiny" they looked. You ask if she'd like to come over to see the actual prints in person. She giggles, looking away momentarily, and purses her lips. She says she's taking the role of your biggest fan if someone doesn't already have it.

When you remember her saying this, you feel the smack of bubblegum sloshing around her purple lips as she adjusts her cleavage in a shirt she swears didn't come from the H&M kids' section.

"Nothing is hotter to me than someone who makes art," she says before leaning in to kiss you.

She tells you all this on your first date.

Later on, you won't know if this *Battlefield Earth* of a relationship not working out is because she cheats on you with a Drake wannabe in Atlanta or because it took her way too long to realize you weren't the guy she fell for in that video.

Back at the office, you pitch a series of application filters that scan your face and can be applied in either video or photo formats. It will be delivered and rolled out in a summer update. It will include updates periodically to coincide with certain seasons and holidays. It'll be "a big hit during Halloween!"

The entire thing is part of a larger package your company submits to one of those big scary intelligence agencies. They're looking at "creative solutions by this century's thought-leaders" to collect data for "undisclosed reasons." They've reached out to you all in particular because "as a company that thrives on the ephemeral, users are less likely to pester officials with tighter regulations and calls for transparency." In return for violating the assumed nature of your company, they've promised a significant slash in your taxes via a provision stashed into a bipartisan bill that will "surely pass before the next election."

They call you guys a "Customer." You call them your "Big, Distant, Dyslexic, Dried Up and Resurrected Rocker Brother."

• •

One night you're both high as gulls with your feet tucked into the maroon sand.

She asks if you know Penny Lane and the Band Aids.

"The girl Kate Hudson plays in *Almost Famous*? Yeah, I know a little about her. Why?"

She tells you how deeply she's wanted to be involved in art all her life. But how badly she sucks at it. She has an eye for what's "pretty or sexy" like Miley Cyrus' bong sculptures or James Franco's paintings but she isn't necessarily good at doing those things herself. She once had an idea to take photos of herself having sex, but from her point of view. You momentarily entertain the idea that this is interesting and innovative. But now she's realized she's far more useful at being close to the epicenter of "where the sexy stuff comes from." A kind of spark plug for the whole process. There's this insatiable lust she has to be in and around a creative environment all the time. Exactly like Penny Lane.

As a result, her New Year's resolution has something to do with fucking hot boys who make good art.

You make the mistake of seeing this as an opening. You begin to chatter on about your unfulfilled and unfinished photo projects as well as the grant proposal which you've been shelving for two summers now. How you wanted to be out traveling, taking photos, and saving the world in the process, instead of being at a tech company. Exactly like Tim Hetherington and Brassai and even Dorothea Lange.

She follows up with an equally horrific truth: her attraction to you has waned because you aren't actually doing those things.

This helps explain her involvement with the generic trap rapper she'd been hooking up with Right Before. They'd also met online. This happened when she was back in Georgia during one of those times she'd returned for an extended period. Initially they were just fuck buddies. But Right Now he is the winding crop circle of a road that all your issues lead back to.

She was just an object for him and she refused to see it as *only* that. Because she knew the objectification was part of it. She was turned on by that part. In his hands she was some kind of conceptual putty. A type of porcelain material that was malleable but still capable of being photoshopped on command. The suggestion of being mastered at another level; of accepting a little too much auto-tune in the amplified pitch that sounds as if it were lifted right out of Young Thug's studio where he calls her moaning "the sound of the South."

All this because they'd fucked in the snow after doing molly and made a few too many jokes about abortions.

How the shit were you supposed to top that?

The empty loft that could fill your unsatisfied dream projects couldn't provide her with anything close to that. So you consider telling her what your *actual* practice consists of.

How your finely tuned 20/20 vision was corroding over the process of staring at bits of HTML every night. Or how it seemed as if your constitution had been further eroded as a result of the charcoal secrets you'd bumped into while navigating heavy waters. And the mass temple of transparency you were the architect of a year ago.

You consider telling her about the uprising you unleashed

and the reasons why you did it. You cancel that thought out as you try to grasp your first evening together under the pier. You're trying to re-hear the tracks of the roller coaster—when it all went silent as she pressed up against you. How it felt uncharacteristically liberating in that meteoric instant. Someone who wanted you. Without the complexities and *maybes*.

How unique it felt in that flash.

Later, you're glad you never mentioned anything; not only because it would've led the FBI right to your door, but because she was evidence that your revolution had failed.

• •

You learn way too much about him. When you're at Joshua Tree for a concert you've scrupulously spent months planning, she unveils that they met only on Sundays to have sex. They fucked in his studio on a tan futon that squeaked at a high pitched increment. Due to its age and constant use it often got stuck in the sofa setting if they tried anything other than missionary. Afterwards, they'd get Chick-fil-A and hotbox his grey fading Subaru. They'd do this all over a hundred times. His recent SoundCloud uploads reference the endless transcendental fucking they unleashed on each other.

You're in a tent together after a long hike on your second day at Joshua Tree. You've made the mistake (again) of assuming this day had been particularly incredible for your relationship when she plays one of his songs on her phone. She stops it after every verse to annotate it. He mentions something about *playing it back again* and she explains that this is a reference to the sex tape they made together. She asks if it would turn you on to watch it.

After all the exuberant fucking, she helped him edit his Post-Trap manifesto via a shared Google Doc. It contained such gems as "Sustainability Rap-Based Musicals Are Dope, Bro."

She never gives any details as to whether this was just a kind of sketchbook for all his thoughts pertaining to the trap scene in Atlanta, or if it's a broader attempt to give the subculture some kind of historical lineage. You assume an overall lack of depth to the project since the music sounds very much in the vein of what literally every single Future wannabe with access to Pro Tools was emoting into the trash island section of the Internet.

Another time following an expensive dinner at a southern restaurant in Malibu you took her to because she was feeling homesick, you wind up at the Ferris wheel. The ride stalls midair with a crystal comatose fog slipping in through the Santa Monica mountains. The exclusivity question is summoned. *This is it, this'll do it,* you're thinking. She mentions how she asked him to be exclusive at one point. He turned her down via a contorted rhyme (that you imagine him reciting as he takes sips from a foam cup filled with codeine) about the oppressive nature of mutually exclusive relationships and how insane it is to assume that a single individual can meet all your needs.

The Ferris wheel loops downward, away from a straightforward answer. The question remains suspended momentarily before leaving you for Topanga Canyon.

• •

Things are never straightforward *good*. There's a lot of screaming in streets late at night. A *lot* of ultimatums. A lot of grey in the conversations following flash-fiction sized paragraphs. A lot of *okays* meant as an ellipsis, but not as a period.

Maybe it would be helped with some straightforward sweaty grinding, you think. But nope, that's not happening Right Now. She withholds and holds and holds and holds and holds. It's some convalescent bullshit, really. First she's not ready. You think it's a matter of winning her over. You take her to shows to see low rent rappers who act like Wiz Khalifa and dress like Doc Brown from *Back to the Future*. You supply her steadily with pot brownies and sex toys. Knowing how much she lives for investigating rap lyrics, you buy Jay-Z's pseudo-biography *Decoded*. When her mom is being an asshole about her overspending her month's worth of money on Smashbox eyeliner you buy her groceries from Whole Foods.

At one point her heart is set on becoming a Suicide Girl. There's a whole process that begins with a themed amateur photoshoot in a specific location. Nudity is not required, but encouraged. She goes on about how an opportunity like this could lead to multiple sponsorships and the possibility of her never having to work retail ever again.

This is the thing. This'll do it for us, you're thinking. You prepare voraciously for this photoshoot skimming tutorials, lighting techniques, suggesting themes and outfits. You lose track of how many naked girls lying in the woods with constellation tattoos she sends you. The two of you settle on a desert island theme. You'll isolate the sandstones and shells of Matador Beach for this. You're directing her into sexier postures with a professional distance. She's entirely within your grasp.

Then she pulls the plug. She asks if you're familiar with Terry Richardson. You say, *Of course.* She asks if you've seen the photos from the Big Leak a year ago—the outtakes where he was in sexually explicit communion with models, lifting girls in the air and eating them out while they gave him a blowjob. You say again that you're familiar with this. You feel this headachy rush as you ask if this is the kind of photoshoot she'd like to do instead.

Before you realized that you were solely a storage space to upload her unedited photos, you entertained the idea of what this could all look like as a permanent thing. You could quit your job and cash out on the opportunity to take semi-nude photos for a burgeoning Instagram model. In between, you'd collaborate with NGO's for projects pertaining to human rights issues. *That would be it. That would do it*, you're thinking.

She shrugs and says that maybe this whole thing was a bad idea.

You realize this plays into a larger narrative of refraining from taking photos with you. She claims to hate selfies. Later when you hack into her iCloud, you know that's not true from the sheer volume of photos she took with her friends back home (and yes, of course, Him as well.) She claims she doesn't want to post anything to social media because her family is incredibly racist and would object to her dating someone who is not white.

This is put further into perspective because it's a family tradition to hang the Confederate flag over the fireplace during Thanksgiving. One of your boys confronts you about the lack of social media activity between the two of you and she drunkenly tells him she doesn't want other guys she might be talking with knowing she's seeing *this guy in red flannels.*

Not long after your failed photoshoot excursion she announces that being a cam girl (aka internet stripper) will be a lucrative source of money. She's always talking about it anyway. About how she'd be great as one of those cam-girls who smacks her own ass and plays with herself for strangers in Croatia. You're concerned about the pervy hackers you know of who exploit idiotic girls like her. You explain politely your concerns regarding internet surveillance and that the best thing for both of your privacy is to place a piece of tape atop both your laptops when they're not in use.

One evening you arrive home to see that your laptop is open with the tape ripped off. She's inhaling the last gram of indica you bought her in a corner on a custom pink La-Z-Boy you bought her. You ask her how long it's been like this.

"I don't know. What's the big deal?"

You yell that maybe she'd understand what the big deal was if she hadn't fallen asleep when you were watching *Citizenfour* a few nights ago.

"Well... so? If more people are watching me that's great! Amber Rose didn't get discovered by hiding at home."

• •

Somewhere in here you burrow into the crystal-emblazoned cavern that reads SEX. But when it does happen, she insists on watching porn on your Samsung 55" flat screen. Maybe it's because she insists on only watching videos with Bree Olsen (*I totally sound like her when I'm being fucked from behind*) or because she still uses His account to do so, but this doesn't really work out for you either. You embarrassingly excuse yourself for being unable to finish much of the time. The few dispersed times you feel the traction on your feet sending shivers into her are cancelled out with a careless comment that you read into as a rogue form of comparison.

"You made me cum. Which is good, I guess," she says.

You think about how she's probably thinking about the time that Fetty Wapp, Jr. over in the South made her cum 14 times in a night. Added to that list of tangential thoughts are the times she talks about him with a kind of late-night-ad spokesperson gusto. Offhandedly mentioning that he should teach boys how to be men. She never mentions that he knows anything about keeping them around, though.

You're not entirely sure if this is coming out as method of catharsis; if you're a therapist or a hole dug up in the desert to stash this all in. She's both equally in need of you and disgusted by this.

••

She goes home (to Georgia) for a bit. To visit her family and settle some things, she says. She swears to you that she won't touch Him. It's just a courtesy thing to see Him and say it's done.

"I won't shave, take a shower, do my hair, or my makeup," she says. You make her promise to text you once they're done hanging out. And she swears (again) that she won't fuck Him.

And you wait. Like you did two summers before. You text her to see if she's gotten home all right. Nothing. You call and leave a sweet message telling her how much you miss her lying on your chest after riding you.

No response.

It's maybe three in the morning and you decide to check in thoroughly. You'd picked up on the password on her phone a while ago. You periscope through the camera to a live feed of her upright because it's already filming.

There are mushrooms, vodka, and the copy of *Decoded* that you gave her in view

"Thanks so much, babe! This is like the nicest thing anyone's ever given me."

"Yeah I thought it would be useful to you."

A giggle. A foot knocks over the bottle of vodka as his hand cups her breast.

"You're my trap queen, you know that right?"

Moaning.

"Fuck me like a little whore, Daddy."

You watch, doze off until about 6 A.M when the sound of flesh flapping together wakes you. You shut it off and slide the video into a folder. You title it *Amateur Atlanta Rapper Gives It to Amateur Muse* and upload it to Redtube.

You wish that had been it. But there's an apology cake she's picked up from Ralphs engraved with sloppy lettering telling you how s-o-r-r-y she is. It's sitting outside your apartment and it looks like the stoner who sleeps under the Venice hostel has dragged his thumb through it.

The tabs of embarrassing shit you'd done to keep her attention are open on your desktop. They appear to be impossible to erase from your history and now you're stuck on another Ferris wheel with her and someone shouts up through a megaphone that the fire department is on the way. She's screaming that this is as good as it's ever going to be for you. You patiently consider jumping off instead of waiting. Instead, you calmly say:

"You're the internet incarnate. Fleeting and indifferent to empathy. Immune to sentimentality. All of life melded into the common rubble of irony. War, sex tapes, Instagram, all reduced to a 140-character sentiment. The daily labor of relationships simplified to a meme with a beach background. All things banal cremated into the form of a hashtag that Amber Rose demanded a fan pay for. Madness in essence. Virulent Madness."

• •

Back at the start she mentions how after seeing Kate Upton's tits in those leaked photos she's convinced more than ever to get her own boob job to make them look exactly like that.

You consider telling her that she has you to thank for that essential revelation.

But you never do.

Someday My Pain

You're staring blankly at a confessional letter with a flickering vertical.

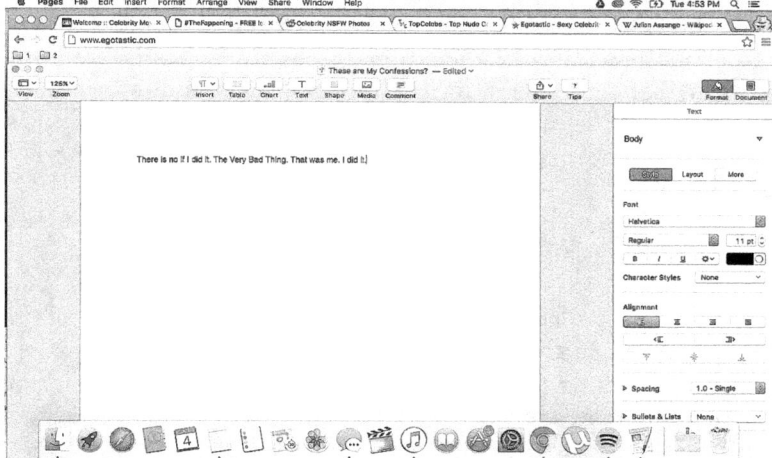

You're attaching a footnote to Marco Reyes' name in the subsequent sentence. The citations page is already quite long, but the anecdote regarding your first hacking adventure will be one that the FBI will use as a reference when they follow up with him for an interview (should they need to).

The anecdote involves poor little sexless Marco Reyes who had a heart as pure as moonshine and loved ginger-haired Jenny Horner. He'd finally shaved off his belly fat and Colombian drug dealer mustache. This gave him the leverage to leap ahead of the other hyenas sniffing at Jenny Horner's polka dot stockings.

Over the course of their tumultuous three month fling, he grabbed her ass at homecoming, brought her Wendy's for lunch, did her social studies homework, took her to softball practice, cleaned her dad's yellow Ferrari, and played photographer for her new looks.

And that puta had to go and cheat on him with Eric Bloshfield.

Things appeared to be hot and fresh between the two as evidence of Marco's stupidly giddy face post-makeout session. He'd sit in Chemistry class afterward, face sagging into the palm of his hand, gawking at the ceiling lights (no doubt replaying the whole thing while trying to readjust his khakis.) But she'd put a major pause on them making it Facebook Official, which at the time, was a big deal (on track to being a possible deal breaker). Who the hell would she be hiding it from? Everyone in the goldfish pond of your senior class knew. Most of the guys had had their passing Jenny Horner moment and couldn't give a shit anymore. The way most folks saw it, Marco had arrived late to a rager that everyone had left.

She'd had a full meltdown the night he asked her why she wouldn't just accept the damn relationship request. She said it was a lot of *pressure*, a lot of *commitment*, she *liked* him *a lot* and wanted to be sure this *special thing* would last. That was Marco's first warning shot.

The next was the time he was midway through looking for a condom in his backpack while Jenny was in the bathroom brushing her teeth. He stopped when he heard her phone vibrate four times. He picked it up, freaking out for a minute thinking it was her dad asking her when she was coming home. He brought it to her and squinted a peek at the name of sender.

"Who's Eric Bloshfield?"

She unwinds with this previously unknown maelstrom of accusations. It goes from her privacy being disrespected to the manner in which Marco is so viciously insecure in his tight Abercrombie jeans because he used to need the relaxed fit.

So he asks you to hack her. Now this was the first time you'd actually considered infiltrating someone you knew. Up until this point, the little hacks you'd done were of the self-serving variety, like auto-renewing library charges and transforming that B- into a B. This was another level.

It wasn't that you didn't know *how* to do it. One lonely summer, you'd consumed one of those old computer manuals and cross-referenced it with the basic coding you and the other kids did back in the Myspace days. Of particular interest was an MIT press handbook called *Access Controlled*, an updated text regarding internet surveillance and the manners in which to circumnavigate this brave new world. You took this as a reverse manual for how an individual could go about doing this. So this was easier than typing.

Even then it was an issue of what might come after. Because Marco was not subtle. He dumped her ass after throwing hot chocolate on her lap in the cafeteria. Out of context, this would appear to be the action of a paranoid boy who couldn't keep it together after a girl touched his penis for the very first time. Which is what scared you. You didn't entirely trust Marco to not be the kind of person to succumb to the pressure of everyone continually nagging him about *why* he dumped her. Under harsh lights, his fragile complexity was keen to the type of social engineering that the FBI uses to get a hacker to spit up info on their buddies regarding encrypted files. A complex program referred to as Rubberhose was introduced in the mid-90s to remedy this type of scenario. It presumed that under threat of bodily harm (aka being tortured with a rubber hose) a hacker would never be able to supply such crucial information because it was deeply encrypted. They would simply and sincerely not know the answer to the question. It was essentially a way of deeply embedding information in a manner that made the answer inexplicable.

Similarly, the answer to the question *Why did you dump Jenny Horner?* would be layered under a pileup of possible scenarios for Marco, such as *What would happen if answering that question meant that you no longer would be passing Trigonometry for the remainder of the semester with a C-?*

Such a program made it possible for you to continue to act in anonymity from there out. It was a system you imposed on all of the virgin Digital Tech 101 slobs who asked for your expertise.

This meant that Marco's entirely intentional action would forever brand him an asshole. He would be the culprit here. Jenny would be the victim because she would have been coldly and publicly humiliated for *literally no reason*. She would wind up taking comfort with Eric Bloshfield over the apparent senselessness of Marco's actions and a kid in her freshman year at UC Davis would be the result.

This kind of scenario (the type where one is left at the metaphorical altar with no handwritten note explaining why) would serve as an origin story for who knows how many people you would surveil through the years.

You'd be able to assemble the necessary pieces to construct a plausible portrait for the reason, but it would never be something that the person being broken up with would be able to perceive. They would have to live with the unknowable. And being the insecure animals that you all are, you'd pick at the biggest scab that equals why (which objectively would not be the reason at all) and scratch away until it was infected with gangrene.

It would be as common an ailment as the flu or student debt.

This ability to *render all transparent* like Dan Dimwiddle would say, would be viewed by most as a type of real-life superpower. But even at seventeen you knew superpowers were as sinful as being gay or an atheist in your rusting town. It would place you in the permanent realm of a social pariah of which there was no escaping.

The ease with which you stick your head under the veil of any of your classmates' interior lives was equivalent to when Clark Kent on *Smalllville* realized he could see through walls. He's playing basketball in the gym, downplaying his strength and abilities already, when suddenly his vision renegotiates the space ahead of him so that there is no barrier. He is no longer looking at a net of boys he could break with a flick of his wrist, but into a girls' locker room. There's an exasperation to realizing he is capable of this and could continue to do this as often as he'd like.

However, his immediate reaction isn't to tell his other buddies what Lana Lang's tits look like. Maybe this is a judgment call he makes because he understands that the human species (which he is not a part of) is weak and horny and would exploit this. Or maybe it's because the most powerful being on the planet is still a teenager, nonimmune to the fear of being drafted into the league of undesirables.

Similarly, your instinct was to downplay this tremendous power by any means necessary.

So, now you're leaving the G-Woman who's reporting all this back to FBI Director James Comey with the big question: *why?*

Well, like you've said, it was about holding onto a set of books just a little longer. Infinitely, actually. But it wouldn't have mattered if it had been a book you would've been able to adjust the price of via Amazon. This, instead, was a reference book that the library would've never let your candy-ass take even to the kids' table: *James Nachtwey's Inferno.*

A photo book tracing the acclaimed conflict photographer's decades-long career, but primarily focusing on his work in Rwanda after the Hutus massacred the Tutsi tribes.

It was a synthetic cocktail of human suffering. Mothers and daughters caught mid-agony, pre-catharsis. Etchings of bones. Pyramids of burned flesh.

The romantic mythos of what a conflict photographer can be felt enlarged.

They weren't the embedded silent flies on the wall, à la Robert Capa catching fleeting moments of mass human error.

They weren't solely diving for cover alongside the troops they were tasked to document. Instead you, via Nachtwey, bore witness to a prologue.

The stillness in the muted draft of an arrangement of malnourished black bodies, some dead, some dying. Naked mothers and children in hospitals. Silent screams in vivid greys. Bones of boys who lie under uncomfortable blankets with flies all around. Scars from brands on backs and cheekbones.

You think you can see yourself in all this. There's a catatonic fog that obscures the whole frame of it but you're certain, even then, that this could be it. You see how being an anti-war photographer has yet to land its mark. The world of conflicts continues to require its intimate witnesses. And you felt with your power to summon peepholes into the pain of others that this is where you would belong. A practitioner of the belief in transformation of suffering into an evolutionary notch.

It's here, where you feel a steady rage—the kind that can sustain something resembling a career—that you first encounter WikiLeaks.

••

On April 5th, 2010, a video that had been leaked by someone in the military was uploaded to YouTube by a website called WikiLeaks. In it, a U.S. AH-64 Apache helicopter circles a compound somewhere in Baghdad and fires at a group of 10 unarmed Iraqi men—killing several civilians and two reporters from Reuters in the process.

You're presenting all of this in a final project for your AP U.S. History class. You've painstakingly taken the time to annotate the video, provide background information on the journalists killed, pull articles from 2007 to demonstrate how the story was originally reported, and most importantly, provide the necessary context to illuminate many of WikiLeaks' other successful informative leaks in order to counteract the narrative that they were solely a crew of anarchist-cyber-hoodlums. You want them to feel this as much as you do, this intangible exasperation for decisions outside their small sphere of the football field.

Ellie Sheever is conducting a vetting process of her prom date. Dominick Falso is stoned and slipping into the crease of his arm. Charles Lee has his first public erection to a set of successfully delivered nudes.

You notice this as you're winding down from a tangent regarding how this moment bears a striking resemblance to the information released by Daniel Ellsberg during the Nixon Administration. The indignation you've compressed into slides brews out, and you declare that subsequent moments of violent secrecy will continue to take place because warnings from whistleblowers regarding the military industrial complex were not heeded in due time. Each Apache helicopter that carries out said attacks may as well have the names of every person in this room on the side of it.

Mr. Tallie stops skimming Breitbart news for a moment, and swiveling around his chair, declares your presentation is over.

Another series of heavy-handed leaks poured out that summer as you transitioned out of the glass bubble of your hometown. The details involve gossipy tidbits revolving around State department and diplomatic affairs. TMZ political stuff, really. But the details that emerged regarding the silvery fox behind it intrigue you most.

In Julian Assange, you find the hero you were never quite ready for. A freak with a freak origin story that felt mythic. His signature mane, retaining its color due to exposure to gamma radiation from a reactor he had improperly reversed the poles on when he was 14, à la Bruce Banner.

A constant nomad. A citizen of only the sublime. His true nemesis: the neoliberal corporate agenda. With a handful of laptops and a few servers hidden in Sweden, he'd rattled the cages of the elite.

There would be calls for his assassination, secret hearings to deliberate extradition for treason, and a thick-as-honey plot to ensnare him in a ludicrous sex scandal. There would be chatter of the Nobel Peace Prize for his website. He's what Sartre would've imagined as the next evolutionary step beyond Che.

There's that fire in your belly that pours into blood in your balls when he speaks of his hobbies which include "crushing bastards." It simmers like a kettle escaping the stove until you wake up one morning in Stanford and the steam from those days of rage comes through like a half-remembered dream.

Your flirtation with a life as a war photographer has crumbled under the weight of certainty that you would be stuck in school for far longer than you'd imagined. Plus, yeah, of course, the debt narrative continues to pick up traction all around.

So you relegate your interests to other places, such as the photography department. You document a brewing social movement curiously calling itself Occupy.

You follow the greasy protesters in their encampments. You become close to them and engage in many spirited discussions about why Ron Paul is the best choice for America. You listen to their stories of how they lost their homes to the banks—defaulting on their med school loans that they took out to join Doctors Without Borders, only to end up a barista at Coffee Bean & Tea Leaf. Your class critiques you harshly for the lack of neutrality present and the manner in which you refer to the struggles of the movement as your own.

You try many different ways.

You start a photo series based on a real life Syrian rebel in Homs. You photograph the grainy cell phone videos he uploads. You include a sex tape you found via dark traffic channels which was used to discredit him previously as leader for the Syrian resistance.

The class believes this is "exploitative" and "profoundly

unsettling... and not in a good way" but also "somehow kinda racist." You rationalize this in an artist statement describing the intimacy found in a sex tape as "humanizing."

You try one more thing.

You take photos of objects from breakups—some your own, some your friends—and ravage them as if they were uncovered beneath debris of a bombed-out building.

You title each staged photo after a major military conflict involving the U.S. This receives criticism such as "offensive," "insensitive," "dour," "disconnected," and "looking for something to be angry at but firing off like an Uzi in all directions."

That summer you're watching a livestream as British authorities prepare to arrest Assange as he awaits asylum from the Ecuadorian embassy in London.

You're working in the IT lab between classes. You're still quite good at maneuvering computers in spite of your art practice collapsing.

Then you're graduating. An academic advisor tells you it'll take five years. The financial aid lady tells you it's possible in four but to expect the job market to be dismal. So you hack it, add a few credits and art electives to your transcript, and make it happen in three.

You're desperate for a job. You see an ad for a summer camp in need of an artist in residence who is good at coding.

That seems like a weird mash-up of things to need, but this is Palo Alto.

You halt a project where you're illegally uploading images from photo books from acclaimed war photographers to JSTOR.

Then you're setting up this odd animated game that involves a Crash Bandicoot rip off character who will supposedly teach privileged 5-year-olds the wonders of coding. In walks this half-drunk sorority chick with long-tequila-sunrise-dipped hair.

Later, you're remotely hacking into the system of a barista from Philz to manipulate a mint-mojito to bring her exactly the drink you brought her that one time.

Then you guys are making out in a closet. You're slipping your fingers into her pants. Children are swarming in and out of the adjacent room as your other hand covers her mouth and a Taylor Swift song you don't know plays all around.

With your metaphorical X-ray telescope, you're looking into the other guy's life. He's sending kissing emojis to a girl who isn't the same one you are mutually attracted to. And she has no idea.

Next, she's telling you that her not picking you at the end of this reality show that your life now resembles has nothing to do with you.

In a jump cut, you're moving in a U-Haul van down south, winding through Big Sur.

After, you investigate the faults Gibson Security pointed out in an ignored memo and become responsible for the information of 4.6 million users being publicly released.

There's someone's mother on CNN crying. The footage cuts back to Ferguson with trash cans on fire.

You're in the office when Tim Cooke releases a statement which says how secure their iCloud servers were. Someone on Twitter comments that this is the corporate equivalent of a company saying that the issue was a stampede of girls with short skirts running around on a big city street.

You're only half-listening because there's a rejection email sitting in your inbox for a project grant you'd recently applied for.

You're watching the FBI through body-cams as they raid some pervy Latino cook on the Southside that you planted the smoking gun.

• •

On October 16th, 1989, NASA was in the midst of a comeback. In the wake of the Challenger explosion which killed its entire crew, the fledgling space program once seen as the brightest beacon of reality in the science fiction realm needed a win.

They prepared for the launch of Galileo on an extended space mission to Jupiter. In order to reach the planet, which was 778.3 million kilometers away, it would need tremendous solar panels. However, NASA scientists decided to bet on a riskier energy source: nuclear. This in the midst of some of the largest anti-nuclear protests occurring on a global scale.

Activists argued that an explosion mid-atmosphere similar to what happened with the Challenger would rain toxic plutonium over the planet. NASA argued that the 50 million dollars' worth of tests they'd conducted in the months leading up to Galileo's launch assured this would not be the case. With protesters lined outside wearing gas masks and clutchhing picket signs, NASA proceeded forward with preparations for the launch on October 18th.

And so, on the morning of October 16th, as NASA staff logged onto their computers and sipped their coffee, a startling message glared at them.

WANK, a worm—a miniature virus—successfully lurked about in NASA servers. A small band of IT techs scrambled in subsequent hours to weed out the hack.

Who could have done this?

Who would have the audacity to take a backdoor channel into one of the most secure government computers on the planet?

The culprits were never apprehended and the launch went ahead as scheduled. Subsequent research into the early years of the internet would point in the direction of a Melbourne-based hacker by the username *Mendax*.

This was the pseudonym of an 18-year-old Julian Assange.

• •

Meanwhile in May 2010, you were sabotaging Ellie Sheever's potential prom date. He was a cheating bastard, but she didn't know that yet.

Truthfully, you envied this fucker. He was the only Dominican kid in four counties, which would've normally opened him up to all the different variations of slurs, but he had one of the highest GPAs in your class and the title of track team superstar. Plus, he was a real charitable shit licker. His sister had Down syndrome, so this gave him carte blanche to volunteer with the Best Buddies program every weekend. His newsfeed was polluted with photos of him with the kids

Ellie went off on Facebook one night in a group IM chat about how his legs could probably crush watermelons. Melanie Lonthill joked that Ellie probably couldn't wait to lose it to him.

Ellie had been a damn good friend for all of high school to you and you'd been wanting to press yourself into her blossoming breasts ever since she announced she needed to up her cup size. You salivated and waited for her to notice that your face no longer had acne marks on it and that you could hold a conversation without averting your eyes to the floor every few seconds.

"You're just so sweet. I'm sure someone will say yes to you!" she says when you ask if she'd consider being your backup date.

One afternoon she receives an anonymous email on her school account while she's in Honors Bio about the Dominican guy's long history of talking dirty to all those younger freshman gals. This after he'd just gathered the gall to ask her to prom that morning. She bolts out of the classroom in tears and doesn't come back until class is over.

It's a week and a half before prom and you've got a grey suit tucked away with a slick purple dress shirt to match her dress. *This'll be it,* you're thinking. Your hands are clammy and you're pacing in the morning before you leave for school, rehearsing how you're going to ask. It'll be a grand total summation of everything. The key to asking her will be in the gesture. You painstakingly glue Oreos (her favorite) to a white slab of butcher paper with the phrase *Prom?* You slip the liner notes of an early Coldplay song to a friend in the marching band so he can do the rendition with a trumpet. Your gesture will sweep her so far off her feet she'll sob with joy at the schlong-slap-in-the-face realization that you were always *The One.* You'll make love for the first time with a John Mayer song in the foreground and spend the summer in an 80s pop song of a romance.

You're holding a set of dandelions and your boys are ready to deliver the ballad. You're waiting for her outside of Honors Calculus, but she's late, which is unusual. You're regretting removing the metaphorical wire-tap you kept on her to track her movements and feelings following the implosion of the situation with the Dominican. Some of her friends scuttle by you and giggle at you adjusting your shirt.

She never shows.

Later you text her to innocently check in. No response. The boys are asking if you're still on to try again tomorrow. *You'll let them know.* You break protocol and reverse the order on the wire-tap.

Turns out the Dominican guy had swooped in last minute and made a show of his vulnerabilities and vices. She found it all incredibly humbling and endearing. Meanwhile there's this hot glue gun wax feeling pouring down your shoulders as you watch this all like a snuff film.

Later, you watch from home as they dance in matching indigo outfits with glitter and embers to a Justin Timberlake song.

• •

Assholes always get more sympathy than they deserve. The entire

28

rationale for this seems to be something that slipped through the cathode rays and latched on to the nervous system of America. The thing being the idea that assholes are redeemable.

This may have come out of some need to explain away the inexplicable. To understand this relatable issue of why these people do and say what they do. And maybe that comes out of the fact that it *is* so relatable. Everyone has an asshole in their life. A work-related one. A friend who always cancels, makes snarky or racist jokes, but retains value by being entertaining in all of this. Usually they're found in someone's romantic life. But they're always supposed to be tolerable and, yes, even lovable once you cut past the layer of fucked-upness.

This propaganda is best reinforced by cable television shows that belong to what critics refer to as the Golden Age of Television. It's a foundation that HBO filled with shows like *The Sopranos* and was later reinforced via steel rods and gorilla glue with the *Mad Mens* and *Breaking Bads* of the world. And it isn't as if this is an innovative concept. Film has capitalized on this with 70s era post-Watergate narratives that were billed as "character studies" (*Raging Bull, Last Tango in Paris, Shampoo*). And we've put up with it much longer when you consider that maybe 1/3 of your Barnes & Noble fiction shelf is filled with writings featuring asshole protagonists written by real-life asshole writers (e.g. Norman Mailer, Charles Bukowski).

Even actual modern reinterpretations of monster films are not immune to this problem. The reboots of these canon narratives always inject a thick layer of sympathy for the monster in question. Their menace and malice is overshadowed by this. Frankenstein is just misunderstood. The Mummy is a heartbroken romantic. Hannibal is in love with his patient (another man) and strays in the direction of eating only those who are rude to him or his friends. Dracula not being able to see his reflection is now tragic because this narcissist is missing out on how pretty he is. In the process of reducing this metaphor to something so superficial, it misses another perfect metaphor that is a universal asshole quality: the inability to see oneself as they actually are.

The worst part is when these asshole narratives are perpetuated by the nerds they used to torture. The same kids who got early acceptance letters into MIT but changed the game last minute to wind up controlling the zeitgeist through the writer's room of

AMC. Can you imagine if someone who'd been illegally detained at Guantanamo for an inordinate amount of time was released, and wrote about how great the meals were there? *The New York Times'* book review staff would publish weekly pieces on the dangers of Stockholm Syndrome. But this lack of awareness on behalf of the nerd cartel controlling cable shows is bound to go unchanged for some time.

Before you'd gone off to commit the heist of the year, there was this Egyptian guy wandering around the office bugging people with technical questions about cybersecurity. He was doing preliminary research for a show of his that had been greenlit on USA network ("The network with that show featuring Tony Shaloub sniffing things?"). From what you overheard, it was about hackers; an "honest depiction" of its subculture. The main protagonist would be this corporate stooge stuck working for this cybersecurity firm whose biggest client was the evillest conglomerate on the planet. It would be a frank depiction of this character's mental state and struggles with anxiety, depression, and drug addiction. You overhear him enthusiastically describing it as a *Fight Club for* the kids who were probably in middle school when it came out." As well-intentioned and earnest as this guy seems, the show already seemed to you unsustainable. This character just sounded sad and pathetic. He wasn't someone everyone would root for week after week because of the level of fucked up things he was doing. Crashing major corporations to cancel debt? Those are things everyone actually wants. But it isn't a compelling-enough premise to most viewers unless he concluded each major (and presumably realistic) hack with a massive orgy of all the board members' spouses.

Audiences want to revel in the despair and vices of their assholes. And showrunners will continue to plummet into their nonexistent depths. They'll play out a season of potential changes for this deeply troubled (usually white male) character and it'll be viewed as "fascinating" and "riveting." But these dickholes don't actually ever change in real life. All of these depictions of them might be getting it close to right (sort of like shaky cam footage meant to mimic documentary techniques) and real life assholes may actually be binge-watching these shows ironically or to stay in the loop. But it never amounts to an actual *change* in persona.

They don't get that enlightened moment where it all just clicks together.

And they sure as hell don't nod their heads with grace as the camera pans up and Train plays in the background. They're just the assholes at the center of their universe.

Eventually it seems like the matching pajama-wearing nerds writing these tales realize in the process that the bad guy can't be allowed to actually leave unscathed. And you, the audience, must be complicit in cheering them on their merry way. Which is why the Walter Whites of Big TV get their brutal reckoning. Because they have to. The linear moral logic of this fictional world must correct itself and dictate a judgment. The chaos must rectify itself. But that rarely translates itself intact here into objective non-television reality. Here, the bad guys get away with it. The series ends when Walter White gets into a van with a new identity because he never does come back to Albuquerque to finish his business. The ultimate failing of these narratives isn't that they're unrealistic. It's that we severely lie to ourselves in the hope that they aren't.

And so, you're crafting an unstable prophecy for all this: that these mismanaged misinterpretations of the complex asshole will meet their ugly end. Maybe in the form of a presidential candidate, a public persona that cannot be ignored by any segment of the culture, that will be considered so deeply dark and irrefutably fucked up that he will polarize every subculture of America. Their dickish qualities would propel them into superstardom at first. But the vetting process of this candidate's past indiscretions would render his asshole-nature so totally transparent that those trying to justify it—in the form of supporters, surrogates, donors, etc.—would reveal who they really were in the process.

And you hope that if a biopic is made of your struggle that, at the very least, they won't cast Shia LaBeouf to play you.

• •

Julian Assange loves bees. He used to keep entire hives of them in his backyard in Melbourne. He was fascinated with their complex innerworkings, the democratic distribution of labor, the organization behind it all. But he also loved their viciousness. Which is why he elected to have them be the protectors of his secrets. He stashed away floppy disks containing information from past hacks (such as the WANK incident) in their hives should the authorities ever track him down. He trained them to not sting him by having them recognize his scent via his sweat whenever he fed them. It was an impenetrable system for which the encryption key could only be human error.

Assange married a young lady and fathered a son with her sometime after the NASA hack. They lived perpetually in motion across parts of Australia like a traveling circus. However, without notice, in October of 1991, his wife left him and took their young son.

A distraught and heartbroken Assange moped around his house for days in a catatonic state. The Australian authorities were on to him following a recent hacking session. He had not been as careful as he normally was of cleaning up after himself. And sure enough, within a number of hours, Australian authorities had followed a series of leads in their pursuit of *Mendax* to his front door. The pirate's loot of stolen information and passcodes that would've normally been stored away in his kingdom of hives was in plain view for them when they arrived.

There are many lessons to disseminate from this when you hear of this anecdote. Namely, that the most important hacker of all-time was not invincible. He was not immune to heartbreak, much like yourself. But more importantly, he was not immune to the scorn of a woman. Calculated and cold as he might come across, here was a man who'd let his shredded atria get the better of him. This had effectively ended his reign as perhaps *the* key player on the hacking scene in the early 90s. This could be attributed to his youth, of course. But women, more than anything, revealed themselves to be this Superman's cancer.

Especially as of recently, of course. The entrapment scenario at play concerning the two women in Sweden who falsely accused him of rape reveals that much. An astute profile of Assange through any intelligence briefing (from a large enough national agency with international ties and resources such as the CIA) would reveal his past history with women and see this as a point of weakness. A trap could be set in the process. A set of allegations in a country that Assange himself describes as the "Saudi Arabia of feminism" would be the perfect setting. None of it would be true, of course. But that wouldn't matter. His reputation would be smeared, and alongside it anything pertaining to his organization and subsequently what his organization had revealed. You can't be a noble liar, can you?

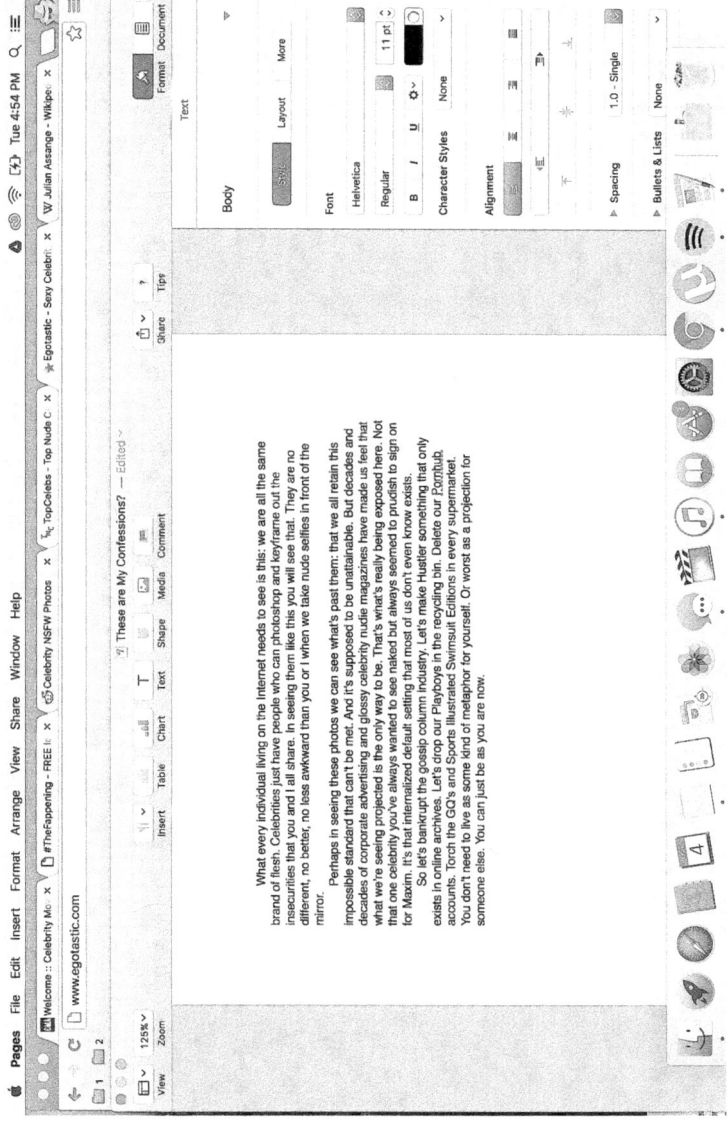

What every individual living on the Internet needs to see is this: we are all the same brand of flesh. Celebrities just have people who can photoshop and keyframe out the insecurities that you and I all share. In seeing them like this you will see that. They are no different, no better, no less awkward than you or I when we take nude selfies in front of the mirror.

Perhaps in seeing these photos we can see what's past them: that we all retain this impossible standard that can't be met. And it's supposed to be unattainable. But decades and decades of corporate advertising and glossy celebrity nudie magazines have made us feel that what we're seeing projected is the only way to be. That's what's really being exposed here. Not that one celebrity you've always wanted to see naked but always seemed to prudish to sign on for Maxim. It's that internalized default setting that most of us don't even know exists.

So let's bankrupt the gossip column industry. Let's make Hustler something that only exists in online archives. Let's drop our Playboys in the recycling bin. Delete our Pornhub accounts. Torch the GQ's and Sports Illustrated Swimsuit Editions in every supermarket. You don't need to live as some kind of metaphor for yourself. Or worst as a projection for someone else. You can just be as you are now.

No one's mentioning how inclusive your selection was. You expected the outrage. But outside of the meninists & Rush Limbaugh, your public support is tepid.

Online though, you are a God to 16-year-old boys everywhere. Bigger than God. Lennon. Bowie. Assange. It gets a catchy name. Something that will never be forgotten. Already the landscape of porn sites has shifted with the massive incision you've carved into the canyon.

Your insurrection is impending and the new twitchy youths clutching at themselves for the first time don't even understand it yet.

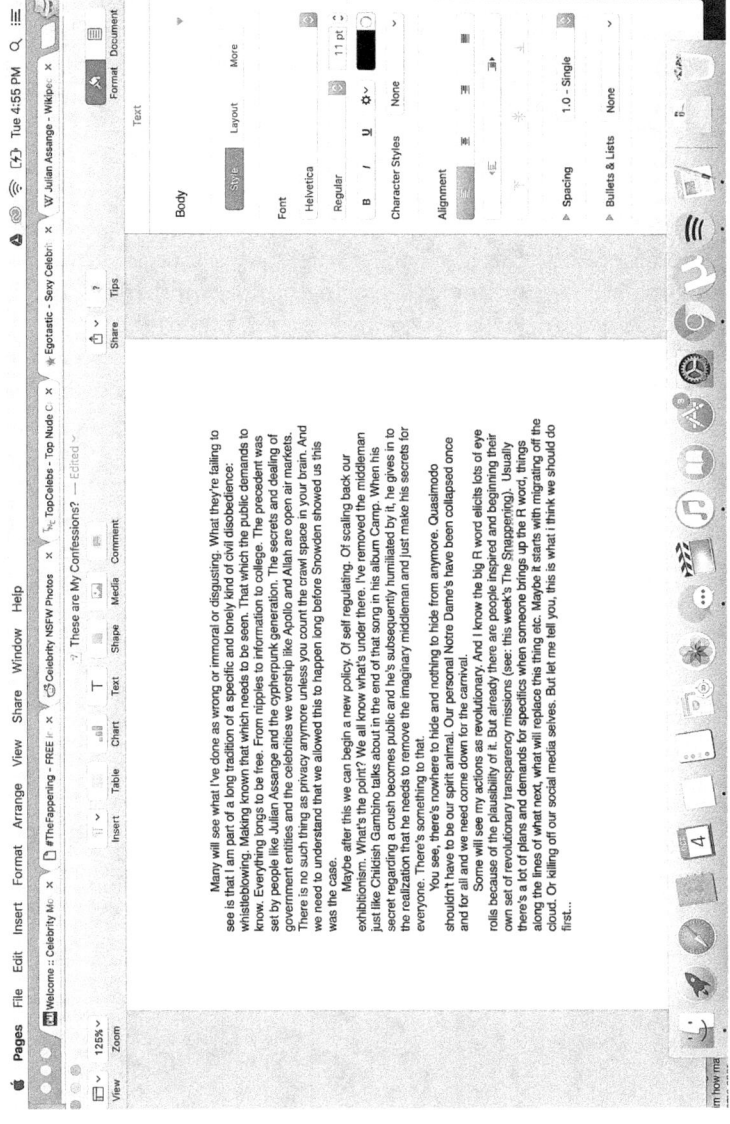

Many will see what I've done as wrong or immoral or disgusting. What they're failing to see is that I am part of a long tradition of a specific and lonely kind of civil disobedience: whistleblowing. Making known that which needs to be seen. That which the public demands to know. Everything longs to be free. From nipples to information to college. The precedent was set by people like Julian Assange and the cypherpunk generation. The secrets and dealing of government entities and the celebrities we worship like Apollo and Allah are open air markets. There is no such thing as privacy anymore unless you count the crawl space in your brain. And we need to understand that we allowed this to happen long before Snowden showed us this was the case.

Maybe after this we can begin a new policy. Of self regulating. Of scaling back our exhibitionism. What's the point? We all know what's under there. I've removed the middleman just like Childish Gambino talks about in the end of that song in his album Camp. When his secret regarding a crush becomes public and he's subsequently humiliated by it, he gives in to the realization that he needs to remove the imaginary middleman and just make his secrets for everyone. There's something to that.

You see, there's nowhere to hide and nothing to hide from anymore. Quasimodo shouldn't have to be our spirit animal. Our personal Notre Dame's have been collapsed once and for all and we need come down for the carnival.

Some will see my actions as revolutionary. And I know the big R word elicits lots of eye rolls because of the plausibility of it. But already there are people inspired and beginning their own set of revolutionary transparency missions (see: this week's The Snappening). Usually there's a lot of plans and demands for specifics when someone brings up the R word, things along the lines of what next, what will replace this thing etc. Maybe it starts with migrating off the cloud. Or killing off of our social media selves. But let me tell you, this is what i think we should do first...

The superhero you've always most admired was The Punisher. Here was someone who didn't hide behind capes or masks or shields. Maybe this was because unlike all the other heroes who don masks to protect their identities, he had nothing to lose. He existed as a result of his family being brutally killed in a mob hit. This pain drove and defined him. It also gave him every reason to fight injustice in a complete manner, not as a half-measure. He was able to exist outside of everything that was normal because he was not and never would be.

You're thinking of this as you're securing money in a digital envelope for Julian Assange's defense fund. Here was someone else undaunted by the terrifying nature of exposure. Once a wild wanderer across continents hacking and exposing corruption every way he went, he was now imprisoned due to ludicrous rape allegations. But he knew this might be the price he would pay. He'd removed the oligarchical middleman from the global conversation: secrecy. And now nothing would ever be the same.

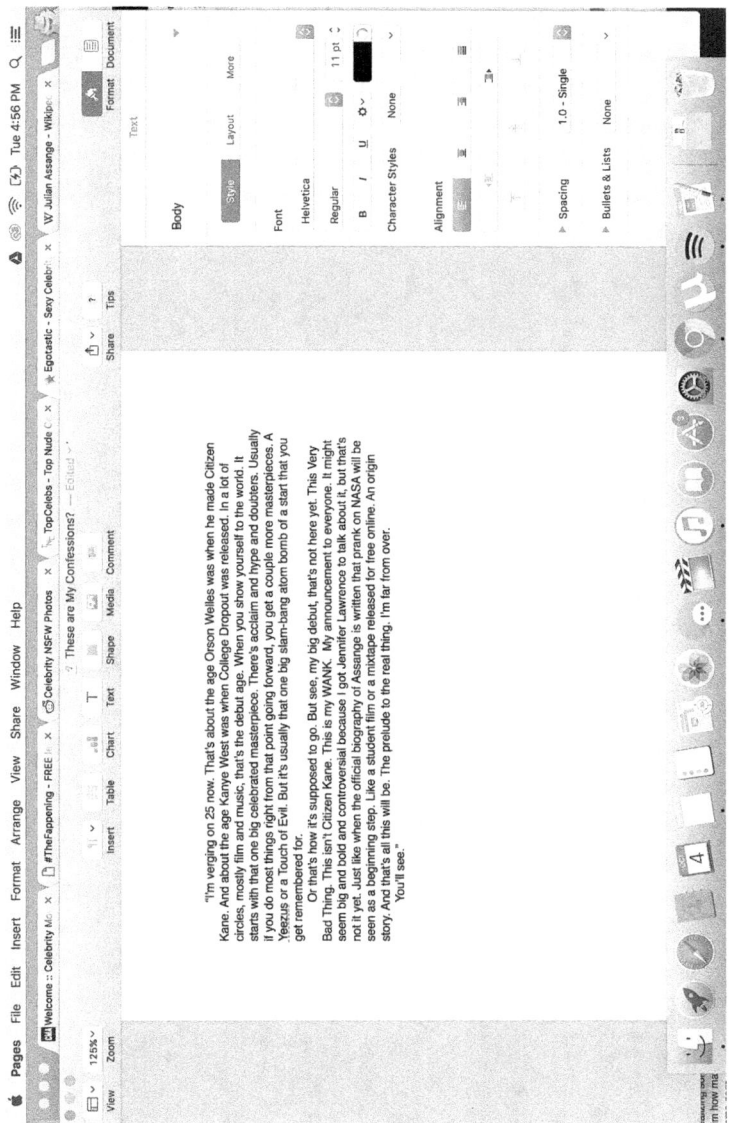

"I'm verging on 25 now. That's about the age Orson Welles was when he made Citizen Kane. And about the age Kanye West was when College Dropout was released. In a lot of circles, mostly film and music, that's the debut age. When you show yourself to the world. It starts with that one big celebrated masterpiece. There's acclaim and hype and doubters. Usually if you do most things right from that point going forward, you get a couple more masterpieces. A Yeezus or a Touch of Evil. But it's usually that one big slam-bang atom bomb of a start that you get remembered for.

Or that's how it's supposed to go. But see, my big debut, that's not here yet. This Very Bad Thing. This isn't Citizen Kane. This is my WANK. My announcement to everyone. It might seem big and bold and controversial because I got Jennifer Lawrence to talk about it, but that's not it yet. Just like when the official biography of Assange is written that prank on NASA will be seen as a beginning step. Like a student film or a mixtape released for free online. An origin story. And that's all this will be. The prelude to the real thing. I'm far from over. You'll see."

You look over the letter for typos one last time and delete it.

IT FAPPENED LAST NIGHT

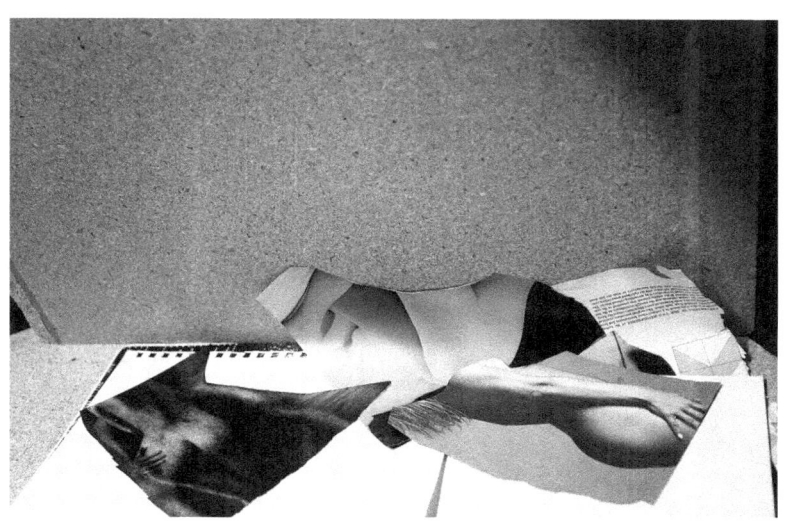

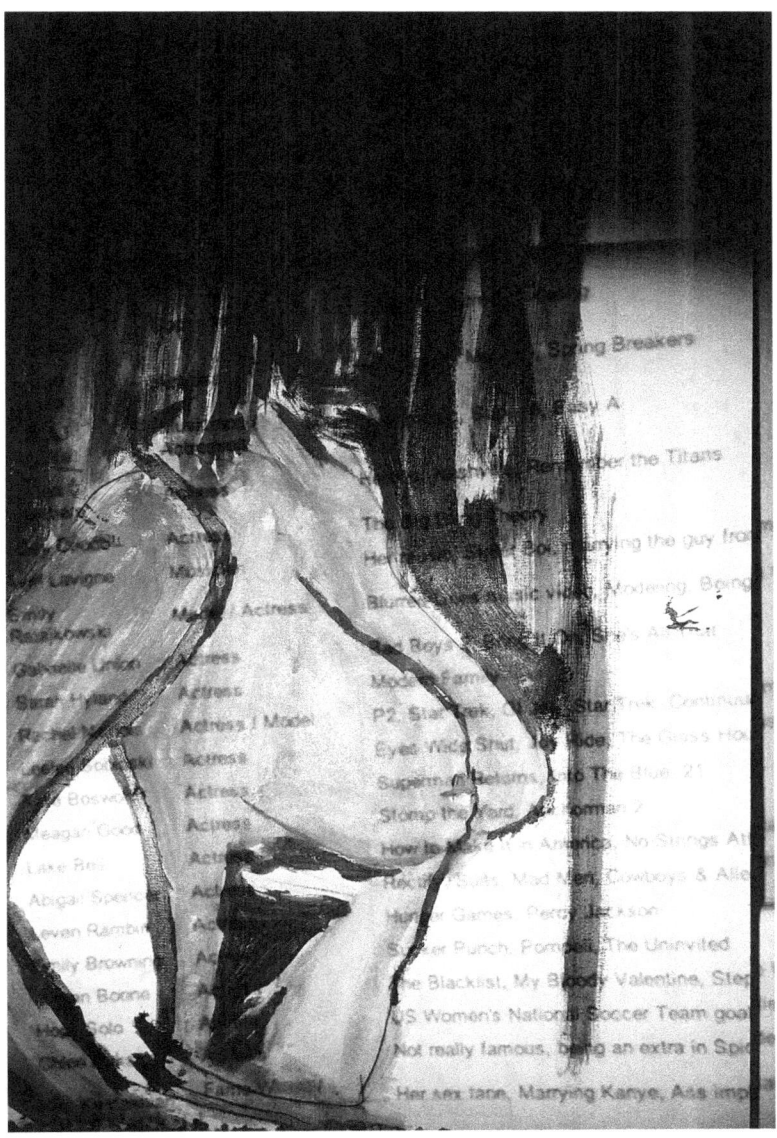

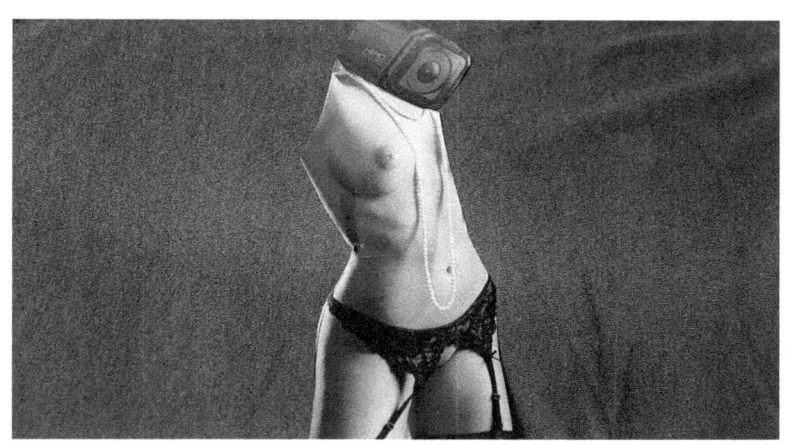

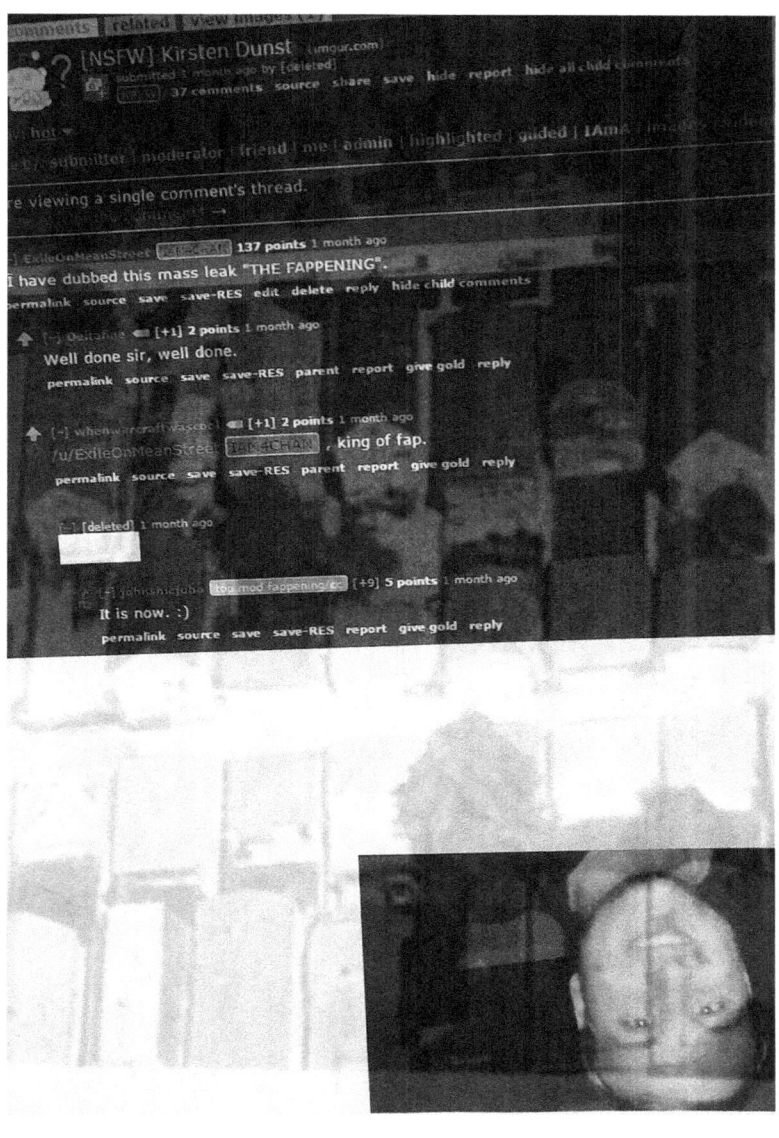

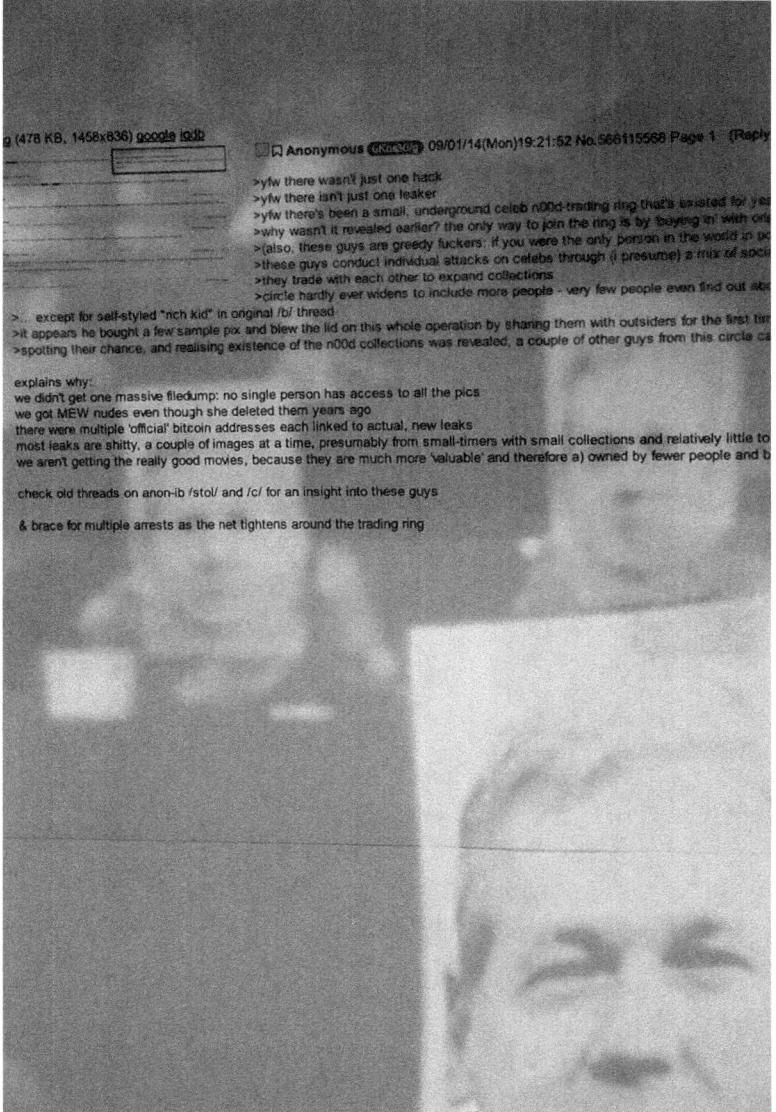

g (478 KB, 1458x836) google igdb

>yfw there wasn't just one hack
>yfw there isn't just one leaker
>yfw there's been a small, underground celeb n00d-trading ring that's existed for yea
>why wasn't it revealed earlier? the only way to join the ring is by 'buying in' with orig
>(also, these guys are greedy fuckers: if you were the only person in the world in po
>these guys conduct individual attacks on celebs through (i presume) a mix of socia
>they trade with each other to expand collections
>circle hardly ever widens to include more people - very few people even find out abo

>... except for self-styled "rich kid" in original /b/ thread
>it appears he bought a few sample pix and blew the lid on this whole operation by sharing them with outsiders for the first tim
>spotting their chance, and realising existence of the n00d collections was revealed, a couple of other guys from this circle ca

explains why:
we didn't get one massive filedump: no single person has access to all the pics
we got MEW nudes even though she deleted them years ago
there were multiple 'official' bitcoin addresses each linked to actual, new leaks
most leaks are shitty, a couple of images at a time, presumably from small-timers with small collections and relatively little to
we aren't getting the really good movies, because they are much more 'valuable' and therefore a) owned by fewer people and b

check old threads on anon-ib /stol/ and /c/ for an insight into these guys

& brace for multiple arrests as the net tightens around the trading ring

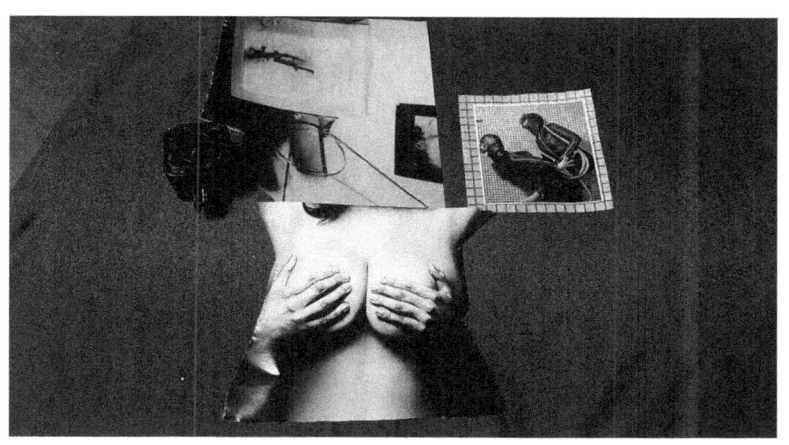

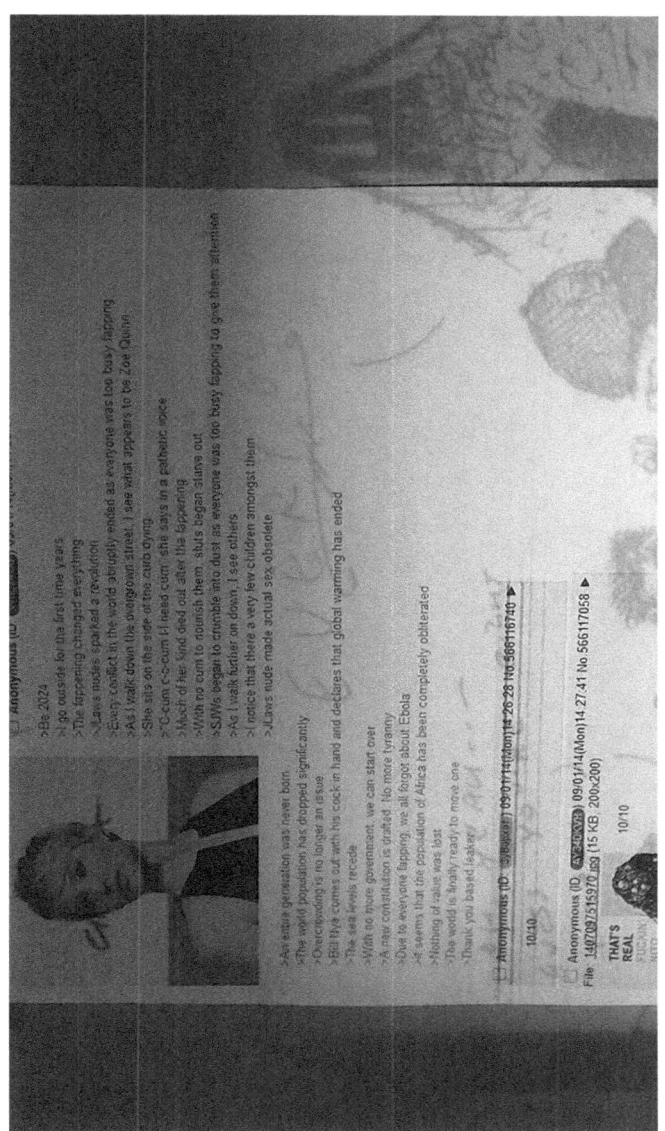

>Be 2024
>I go outside for the first time in years
>The happening changed everything
>Jews nudes sparked a revolution
>Every conflict in the world abruptly ended as everyone was too busy fapping
>As I walk down the overgrown street, I see what appears to be Zoe Quinn
>She sits on the side of the curb crying
>"C-cum c-c-cum if I need cum! she says in a pathetic voice
>Much of her kind died out after the happening
>With no cum to nourish them sluts began starve out
>SJWs began to crumble into dust as everyone was too busy fapping to give them attention
>As I walk further on down, I see others
>I notice that there a very few children amongst them
>Jews nude made actual sex obsolete

>An entire generation was never born
>The world population has dropped significantly
>Overpopulation is no longer an issue
>But I've come out with his cock in hand and declares that global warming has ended
>The sea levels recede
>With no more government, we can start over
>A new constitution is drafted. No more tyranny
>Due to everyone fapping, we all forgot about Ebola
>It seems that the population of Africa has been completely obliterated
>Nothing of value was lost
>The world is finally ready to move one
>Thank you based leakery

10/10

Anonymous (ID:) 09/01/14(Mon)14:26:28 No.561116740 ▲

10/10

Anonymous (ID:) 09/01/14(Mon)14:27:41 No.561117058 ▲
File 140709731597G.jpg (15 KB, 200x200)

THAT'S
REAL

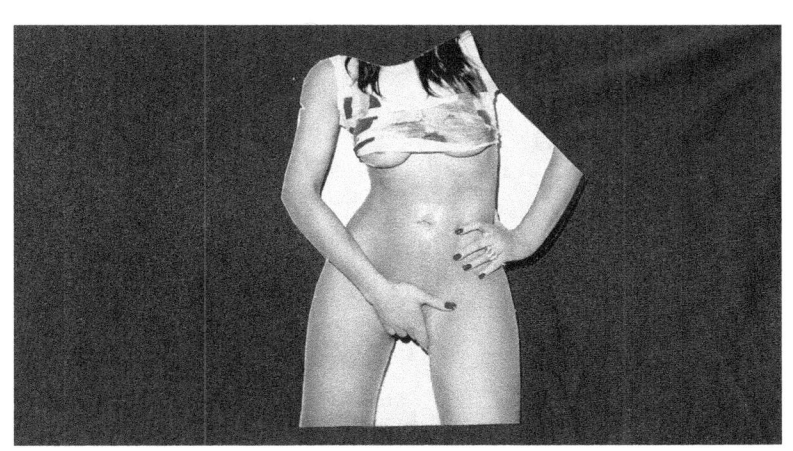

SILICON BEACH

The lanes are too narrow for buses, public or private. The only way out is by entering a stockpile row of cars forming waves filtering onto Venice Boulevard and Ocean Avenue. The sidewalks to walk along these widened alleys that developers call canals feel like slabs of leftover sheetrock.

There's no evidence of space existing for several people to walk side by side as they crawl out and face South Venice. Instead the closest thing placing things of permanence next to what will inevitably slip past is a complex with a poster of Che trapped in a window next to a television set that seems looped on Fox Business.

Your late-aughts-era condo placates itself at the rim of one of these canals. Its proximity to Mao's Kitchen is what drew you into dropping your post-college savings. All that summer camp money existing here all at once.

This proximity means it's also dutifully close to the office. This is quite a good thing in fact because you were briefly concerned about having to buy a car when you moved back down here. This, comprised with how you are somehow convinced that your neighbors have to pay other people to move their cars so they won't lose their spots, makes you #grateful.

But navigating these portals which look like hexagon swimming pools in grid mode via Google Maps is sure as hell not easy. One morning, staring into your phone, you almost walk into oncoming traffic.

Another morning you're somehow all the way by the Hot Dog on a Stick stand below the Santa Monica Pier.

"We know you're new to the city and still maneuvering around, but please don't let this become a habit," they say.

"We're really gonna need you once the expansion starts happening later this year!"

"This is probably a little too candid, but we know you're going to be an essential part of how this company reimagines itself."

"Your background in the arts gives you a lot of room to shape how this company portrays itself aesthetically."

"And subsequently how people take those aesthetics into their own lives!"

"Right! It's going to differentiate us from everyone else because those aesthetic choices are going to shape the next ten years or so."

"Everyone who has a smartphone will communicate with *us* as the delivery system for those communications!"

"Those aesthetics are going to leak over into every decision they make whether they're rational, spontaneous, or ethical ones."

"Aesthetics are going to influence ethics!"

"Yup! Yellow is gonna unseat the Blue!"

"Right! And we're gonna make that Jesse-Eisenberg-look-alike-motherfucker eat his stock over spoiled kale salad!"

"Three Billion Dollars isn't enough to buy our creative potential!"

"Anyway, we really want you to enjoy the rest of what's left of this summer!"

"Oh, and again, we're super happy to have you!"

That was the same summer that everything looming underneath your feet would rise to permanence. When the fragments of your thinking about what constitutes a rear window were spliced into something that you swear was plagiarized from a fictional speech.

That's the summer that a nerd working for the NSA revealed that the Gene Hackman's of the world were more right about things than anyone ever hoped they would be.

That summer your steed, Rocinante you called her, roared with the budget of a getaway romance hoping to find its funding along a Half Moon Bay highway. There was the anticipation that you'd be able to chase the lust and longing out of yourself. Maybe if you hit a deer. Or felt a swarm of ticks along your leg that resulted in driving off a cliff to catch the sun setting.

This summer that you were now being asked to finish enjoying was the one which put you into the category of Bay Area refugee.

It was the summer you learned that Orwell had gotten the year all wrong.

• •

You're making friends with the boys, though! Quickly, too, because somehow you're capable of putting all that inessential stuff from Back There under a pound-cake's worth of self-deprecating humor.

"Yeah, man, why would I wanna be tied down anyway? There's so many hot-ass chicks here in L.A.! We would've had to do a long-distance thing 'cause no way was I gonna stay up there. Fuck that! And she had a nice ass and was a solid kisser and all but she was a little too round for me. I kinda prefer blonde chicks who aren't into Bon Iver, anyway."

That's what you say in variations when you're asked about what's Back There. It gets you going for long whiles when they prod it out of you, usually with something alcohol-related. You never go full Fredo Corleone and rat it out, though. That would be unseemly. This reluctance gives you this wounded shelter dog quality which quickly makes them want to adopt you into their fold.

"You're a nice guy, man! It's your best and worst quality," they're saying.

The Boys turn you into a special project of sorts. They advise you on the best stock to invest in. The best apps for ordering food when you're too stoned to leave the apartment. The best museums with the most aesthetically pleasing artworks to take a profile picture in front of.

But mostly they're adamant about finding you a new girl.

"Fuck the first one you set eyes on."

"Even if she's a grenade."

"Doesn't matter if her ass is a dashboard, just do it."

"Don't worry about not being as good-looking as that V-necked mountain man!"

"Yeah! You've got good intentions so that counts for something!"

You watch the boys at play in this arena. You're an amateur zoologist here. Observing mating habits. Materials and gestures to mimic. The delivery of this information is both through firsthand accounts but primarily through secondhand recounted tales of debauchery that almost always end the same way: ejecting the escape pod out of the life of whoever they'd been sleeping with. It didn't matter how long it had been, whether it was once or once a week. There was a clear escape route carved out that involved eradicating any way for the other party involved to ask follow up questions. It was an ironclad, Soviet-esque arrangement where questions were met with propaganda-esque answers like, "That's just how it goes."

You're at the Bungalow. One of the boys (who looks like a guy you remember from high school who used to always have his locker zip-tied shut by the guys on the basketball team) is finishing one of these stories. There are cushions being tossed, ping pong balls landing in soil, and gaggles and gaggles of gals making an entrance.

You've got this.

You're sent on a scouting mission at the end of the bar to refill that yellow skirt's glass. You remain in range while they fill a public observation deck.

You're trapped in a long-ass line because the intoxicated girl at the end is attempting to get the bartender to invest in her new app (something about tinder for girls) which she swears will be a hit, in order to get out of paying for her drink.

And so you walk over behind the yellow skirt when it's her turn. And you breathe heavily. Not like in a Helga Pataki's stalker kinda way, but heavy enough that a few volume notches down and everyone would know you were this fucking nervous because you're also ruffling your shirt to make sure the sleeves stay folded up because they never do.

You've definitely got this.

Now's the wrong time to check to see if you have cash instead of card on the off chance that their Square app acts all funky, so you're fumbling through your wallet, feeling around to make sure you tucked a condom behind your ID when your phone vibrates and you check for the fourth time that night just in case it's Her telling you she's spotted you from the other end of the room and she's there because she made a terrible mistake picking the other guy and she wants to be with you and only you and then you're hoping this part doesn't happen until after you've started chatting with the yellow skirt so that She can see you two talking and feel justifiably threatened because Holy Huell Howser is this blonde's ass perfect and She would be understandably taken aback and maybe even momentarily heartbroken in the way that the other person is in a movie like *Hitch* when they think they've missed their shot only to be proven wrong at the end because the two leads *have to* end up together no matter what and it occurs to you that you should hurry this plot point along and talk to this girl with the perfect ass in front of you, but she's already left anyway and this isn't the last time this happens to you.

"Maybe try one of the apps, man."

"I know a guy who was having his dick sucked like 40 minutes after he matched with someone."

You work through the questions in the About Me section, but always have trouble truthfully answering them. Interests? What's someone supposed to say to that if they aren't a surfer or Anthony Bourdain?

Instead you and the Boys, who seem to come from this place

where only flip flops and dazing off in slurs happens, stumble this particular Friday into another Saturday.

You're in West Hollywood. Actually, Westwood.

That's Thursday. This is Friday and you're still hungover when the Uber shows up late.

You run out because one of your friends is throwing up and you're tripping on some ecstasy that your coworker's roommate Sheila gave you

But that's not the reason exactly that you're tripping out of some Armenian guy's Prius and staring into the mirror of a heavily-tattooed guy's condo not remembering exactly why you're there or why there's blood leaking out from the back of your skull or why your hands are covered in dirt and moss.

• •

The office is packing itself up to move out to new offices on Abbot Kinney. You've only been in this beachfront house a month or so, but you were really starting to like it. There was this lingering stench from the marijuana dispensary that once stood in its place. There was graffiti in one of the bathrooms with big checkered-off signage from when Nike used it as a party house.

You're asked to play-test an upcoming update.

It's a new feature with a more literary appeal that will essentially make linear all the grainy memory sequences of flesh hustled back to each other.

It's a way for users to take control of their moments and create a chronological narrative of a ski adventure, a rock climbing trip, an ordinary day into something that is their own. It's something that will expand in future updates so that users can check-in to see snippets of a live event such as a concert or when the Ball is about to drop in New York.

It'll be especially useful as a delivery system of sorts during the next election season.

You'll be in a room with the Democratic candidate speaking from somewhere in Nebraska and 20 seconds later right next to the Republican Vice Presidential candidate leaving an event in Cincinnati. It'll be a utopia of opinions.

So you document your routine.

You film your walk across the canal extra early in the morning when there's still that grain of purple hanging on to the acid modern house.

There's one with text aligned parallel to a particular crossbred Chinese linoleum stone house.

There's another with a set of skaters cruising by into a fold of pigeons. There's a shout-out you include to California's greatest governor.

Then you're eating a sandwich in the bleachers watching a 60-something dude lifting as he adjusts a Duran Duran track on his taped up boombox.

You try out the new spinning green hand-shaped chairs in the office. There's a bunch of thumbs up photos from the other guys signifying approval over the new latte maker which downloads recipes online in real time and takes those orders verbally.

You're cheering with the boys holding margaritas in short rim glasses on the balcony where Jim Morrison once threatened to leap off if Ray Manzarek didn't join the band.

You're back at Mao's Kitchen for the second time that day holding up a copy of *The Communist Manifesto*. Overall, the whole ordeal is about 155 seconds, video and photos in all. Which is a lot more than, say, Chris Wertzner was able to gnash together when it was his turn to do this last week.

There's a lot more stuff you leave out but that's because it wouldn't make for the "exciting glimpse into one of the fastest rising creative startups NOT in Silicon Valley" that was expected of everyone.

It's the kind of boring shit you're actually doing when a buddy you haven't seen in a while calls pleading for you to come out and do some coke at the Echoplex and you decline because you say you have food poisoning from bad Korean barbecue.

Those small shameful loops that you start to enjoy because they start to be painted into the pattern of your day. Like maybe having to wait for the hot water in the shower or stepping over the spot where the dog likes to shit which takes over half the Venice sidewalk. Or those bouts when you find yourself crying after you've smoked a bowl and ground up some Benzos. And how you can't watch The Graduate or Harold and Maude anymore without sticking your fingers in your mouth to dry-heave.

In the sitcom version of your life, this would be edited into a montage sequence that would elicit sympathy from viewers. It would be viewed as mildly hilarious but achingly honest, as well. After a particularly humiliating incident involving your coworker discovering your massive porn collection, it would conclude for the season finale on what would look like the beginning of a turnaround.

You start a reddit account one evening when you're too drunk to sleep. You start off having several usernames to troll folks who like to post things in the New American Right section. Your initial shock over the number of seemingly well-educated people who believe the president was not born in this country wears off. It becomes a contest of sorts. To out-crazy the casual psychopaths. You create forums within forums. They push a theory you popularize that the root of Obama's rage toward the white middle class is the fact that he is the bastard child of Malcolm X. This becomes a well-adopted theory that is taken off reddit into chat rooms that you moderate as safe spaces for depraved conspiracy rhetoric. Racial epithets are common. As are vivid and depraved sexual descriptions of what can or should be done to liberals like Obama. (Hillary Clinton is another favorite target for this.)

These people work in fast food. In saw mills. In cramped offices. Just like you.

Well, not *just* like you.

You let slip where you actually work once to these subhumans and someone refers to it as "normalizing the foul practice of sexting." This person is probably a virgin. He (because he is most definitely a *he* and you don't even need to dig very deep into his life to know that) has never and most likely will never receive a sext in his life. He backs all this up by talking about Jesus and the sin of self-pleasure. Someone (aka *you*) say to him, "Bro, do you even know where you are? The Internet is like Gomorrah."

He responds that he's there to make sinners like you see the error in their lifestyle choices. His cause would appear admirable, if misguided, but his constant references to Latinos as Biblically proven subordinates derails whatever minuscule rationale there is to his arguments.

In the process of planting child porn onto their IP addresses so that you can alert the FBI, these True Americans accidentally drop you into the land of 4chan. There, in the black pond, where rifles are traded for ecstasy, you crouch inside what you can only visually describe as a perpendicular hallway of female anatomy. But a very specific kind.

The forbidden ozone layer of celebrity skin.

It's the shock and thrill of the uncertainty attached to the contemporary. They are behind the grey glass curtain where things are supposed to stay unseen.

You aren't supposed to be here.

And they can never tell. It becomes increasingly straightforward to convince a Disney Channel actress you've always clamored for that she's been locked out of her Gmail and that only through your skilled protection and guidance can she be redeemed.

Your primary account for this illusion of redeemer is appleprivacysecurity

You wait patiently, bait cast, hand adjusting your metaphorical Cabela Pro fishing line. And she sinks her teeth in.

The common assumption of the free-floating nature of metadata is that it is an ocean. A liquid realm. This is correct, but also mildly inaccurate. It best resembles water vapor suspended above you; an aerosol wall of frozen droplets forming a black sea above us all.

You jump into the troposphere. She drags your bait into the under/over-water castle with glass door frames.

Peering through each passageway you catch glimpses of the properly manicured bits arranged for a Vogue photoshoot. They give way to an orange hue of a self-portrait with facial cleanser in a bathrobe.

You emerge to the surface a liberator of the untouched RAW flesh.

You don't ever quite flip and sell to just anyone who asks what you've got. You mostly just collect. You brag to fellow redditors that you've got a "trove like you wouldn't believe" and this becomes more true in ensuing months. Some less-than-below-average schmuck in Pennsylvania starts listing off names that you couldn't possibly own, but to his dismay, via an encrypted TOR transaction that later you will re-route back to his eCommerce employee server, he discovers you have them all.

He refers to you as the xKeyscore of celebrity porn. He asks if you take requests.

And this becomes your Wall.

You listen to a lot of Pink Floyd during that time as well which you consider ironic but not related to this situation exactly. It's a way of fencing out latent sexual appetites. Of containing a set of impulses that go unmet. You're reaching sweet, sweet release night after night to a set of covert access points.

Goddamn, how it's been awhile.

You'd stored it all away for Her all summer. You weren't necessarily thinking of that as something to check off a list, but it was certainly on your mind.

And you kept saying, "It's worth it, it's worth it, it's worth it" to convince yourself to just hold it all in so that when it did finally happen, all the gravitas and manpower put into the heist of a lifetime would make it immaculate.

But that never came to be.

Her last words to you in person just sort of hung over you like that awful handwritten banner in the new office.

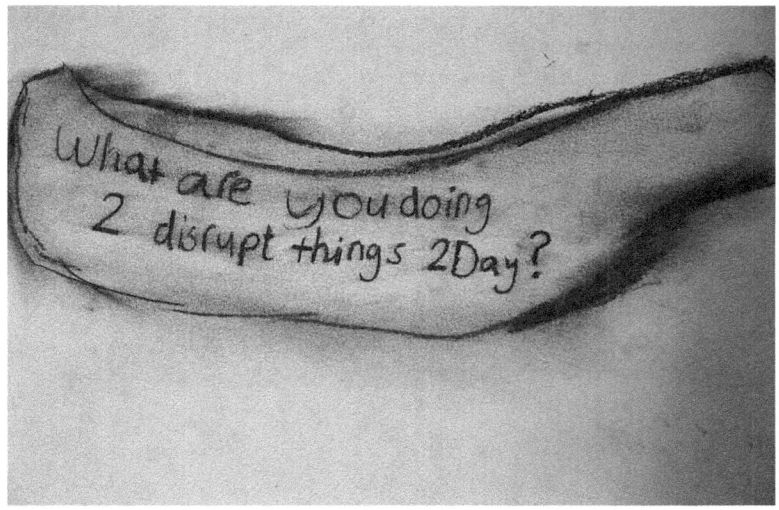

You're thinking of this as you prepare a candid and graceful response to an Anna Wintour wannabe's questions regarding your company's approach to privacy.

You smile and say, "Everyone has a rear window now in their pocket. That's where the revolution has brought us."

THE GIRLS OF SUMMER

80 - I've settled on our genre.

79 - We're lovers on the run.

78 - Perpetually moving.

77 - On a consistent high-speed-sub-machine-gun-clad chase away from the rumors of responsibility.

76 - Every loud, potentially uncalibrated step meant to elude the forebears of age and time.

75 - Our guns blaze across the sunbeams emitted from our convertible.

74 - Bullets are stashed for those who dare question the authenticity of our youth.

73 - Every attempt to tame us met with the answer of our insatiable commitment to each other.

72 - Hotel room beds devoured to prove it.

71 - But it's no matter—we'll learn to mend them in the iron-casting class we'd take on the way.

70 - Deserts, range upon range of mountains, bellies of awful blue sky, valleys displacing into signposts with lizard kings standing on them.

69 - All swinging by us as we tear through road maps.

68 - We're on the way to Paris. No, Dublin. Mexico City, rather.

67 - We don't have the blues, but we're running like we do.

66 - We cut through a small town reminiscent of both our homes along the way.

65 - In a slow-motion sequence we take the Bank of America by charm and wit.

64 - The tellers laugh at us, applauding us, handing over the money Goldman took on loan.

63 - Another night, while you're sleeping like a casual burrito,

62 - I steal away to a vault on the Paramount Lot and snatch a 35mm copy of Harold and Maude.

61 - We project it against a series of boulders in Joshua Tree.

60 - They definitely won't let up on us after that.

59 - You're telling me no romantic gesture, no matter how grand it may seem, is worth the fury it would hurl back at us.

58 - And I just sit back, turning up our playlist to carry over the tunes of the police sirens.

57 - Ours is not solely a lustful reign of fear and mindless anarchy

56 - It is one passionate engagement of our surroundings,

55 - Of the pre-teens who clamor for views of our impersonations,

54 - Of impossible renditions and reenactments of *Our Town* & *Once* done with a time-travel twist.

53 - We engage and entertain our local populace, charming them into submission.

52 - Our collaborative components slow-churning the lemonade.

51 - You, with your hair-tossing charisma and magnetism, and Me, with my self-deprecating elongated stories of times that mattered eons before you.

50 - Hell, we'll even document all of it, those creeps on the NSA switchboard be damned.

49 - Every eroding aching step.

48 - All those night moves through offbeat paths with soundtracks of dad rock and choirs of acoustic gentlemen.

47 - Every one of our hidden gestures harkening to secret transparencies that no documentarian can bear witness to.

46 - Our reign draws to an end when drones whistle into the landscape.

45 - We don't hit the ground together like we're supposed to.

44 - In the fallout, there's smog from revolvers and new regulations in place.

43 - I slip loose from the arresting officer's trunk and redirect Forward, promising a reunion.

42 - "Don't worry," you keep saying. "It's a good thing."

41 - I still don't know what that means.

40 - I swerve through the vultures on the road when one of them drops a letter into my window.

39 - Like lovers in wartime, you update me on your progress.

38 - Shackled to the lines of responsibility and normality, you tell me of your punishment in the form of being forced to marry the town real estate boy.

37 - We continue to exchange letters across enemy wiring.

36 - It all remains afloat so long as it retains tangibility.

35 - It is an unspoken promise of return.

34 - Of not a maybe, but when.

33 - In the meantime, sugary coffee and cherry pies at diners with flirty waitresses will suffice.

32 - Missions remain unclear.

31 - As do the deer hurling their young through leaves and blades of loveless haze.

30 - Nights wander uphill drunk into the morning suns.

29 - I'm waiting with reporters from Reuters for Snowden and we're taking bets on which one of you will show up first.

28 - Months fold into one another with the hustler train passing through every available space.

27 - In a dream where we're both wrapped in silicon you ask me, "Have you ever been out of yourself?"

26 - Two months later at a BP gas station with fauna and fluorescent lights I realize you never came with me.

25 - You stayed back there, back then, and the soundtracks that we'd scavenged together were only what I'd imagined you would listen to.

24 - The possibility emerges that I have been diagnosed with the decade-old Latin American Curse:

23 - of shadow above substance,

22 - of temporality than permanence,

21 - of a casual want than a desired need.

20 - I'm, after all, the one who'd most certainly have led to a shared demise under a hail of moon-dipped bullets.

19 - The form of all of this is called into question

18 - I'm no longer raging across highways but stampeding through a keyboard at 2:46 in the morning in the labyrinth of this all.

17 - The Prism we're both lodged in exposes the loop of looking that we've confused for exorcisms carved into the clouds with a Boeing jet.

16 - But this particular attempt will be the grand dragnet to snatch the General-All-Of-It.

15 - The mess and coffee stains of its gorgeously clad entirety.

14 - This will be my wine drained, CinemaScope, 70mm, *Once Upon a Time in America* style Epic.

13 - A Western. No, a Noir. In the subcategory of Sunshine and Surveillance. A tale of love with no regret. It'll best summarize it all.

12 - It'll Fail. But it'll also be the Last of Them.

11 - Seasons collapse into one another

10 - Beaches are abandoned

9 - Campsites dismantled

8 - RV's with Dead-Head stickers refill their tanks.

7 - The sun that always caked us over the inflatables crosses over to the blacktop one last time.

6 - With the Don in the front seat and a handful of gentlemen ready to deliver to you the a capella version of the Anthem-Of-Return,

5 - We drive by your house,

4 - And like Don predicted,

3 - You're not home.

2 - I let out the boys of summer on the corner.

1 - And in reverse, I'm on the road to an unknown beach in Buenos Aires.

3D PRINTED BRANGELINA MASK

If you're reading this now it means I had the audacity to send it, so hopefully that means you have the temperament to read all of it. Please, please don't take any of this as me trying to have the final word here. I know you said you never wanted to talk to me again and that you hated me, but it doesn't seem right to let it end there. We were good to each other most of the time. And I really, really did like you.

But I would be doing myself a huge disservice if I didn't say a few things which I think you need to hear. However harsh they may actually come across.

I don't want to spend the five minutes or so that I have your attention relitigating all our fights but it's become increasingly clear to me that you may *need* some of those moments replayed in full.

I don't think you're a bad person. But Jesus, do you have some fucked up views about women. And it's better you hear it from me than someone who is a little more militantly feminist and will legitimately not hesitate to kick your ass.

No one is obligated to sleep with you because you're a nice guy. No one. Period. And for that matter buying someone expensive and well-thought-out gifts that you qualify as "gestures" doesn't make you particularly nice. I know you think wanting to go out of your way for girls you're attracted to makes you different from the fuckboys who don't, but that's just not it.

I don't think you see those qualities in yourself. You're always trying to go out of your way to separate yourself from those douchebags.

I'm getting ahead of myself, though. We were good to each other much of the time. But I'm afraid I'll look back in a few years and realize that it was more fighting than us actually being happy. So maybe clearing this out now in this manner will make it possible for me to forgive you for some of the things you did.

Okay I'm sorry, but those masks. The really expensive 3D printed ones you had done in Culver City. They're really creepy.

Please don't ever ask another girl you have sex with to wear those. They might threaten to have you arrested, or run away after macing you.

At first I thought that it could be really sexy. Impersonating celebrity couples. Yeah that was kind of a hot idea. And you were right, they were pretty lifelike, but not in a super hollow way that made them look like you were sticking your head in a jack-o'-lantern. They were really sexily made and felt kinda like silk instead of rubber, which was interesting.

But that can't be the only thing that turns you on, right?

In a way, I feel kind of bad calling you out on this. It's almost cruel. If that's your thing and it turns you on, okay great! Maybe you aren't the only one, and I really do hope you find someone who is.

I just don't think that's it, though. It's too specific a *fetish*. That's why the porn freaks me out so much. Yeah, I know what you're going to say. Everyone looks at it. Yes, me included. It makes many a boring night at home after a bottle of wine okay. I admit that. But this is maybe the storage locker equivalent of porn. And I asked my friends about it because I really, really wanted to be okay with it at first. Maybe I could look at it with you? That was my first thought. And it's not a fucking jealousy thing. I swear.

It just started to occur to me that mask or not, you were never actually having sex with me. Of course, there's no way to prove this. You'll deny it to yourself, to anyone who asks. But it's just not possible. You had this infinite gold mine of celebrity tits to shuffle through in your head whenever we were having sex. After I stumbled onto that, I couldn't get that thought out of my head. That no matter how great the sex might be in that moment, you just were never *there*.

I don't know if that started when we were dating. It probably started a while ago. I also don't know how many of those photos you obtained illegally, and honestly the answer to that terrifies me. And I know. Me moving out here to Norway probably made it worse. Whatever intimacy we had was reduced to jerking off to pixelated versions of ourselves. The first time I came back to visit was when I first noticed it. You just weren't present. And after finding your porn stash, I don't know if you ever were.

I think maybe working in the tech world makes you think that people are just accumulations of likes and metadata. But that's not true. There's so much more under all of that. Little details you can't share and capture. And I know what you're thinking. That it's incredibly hypocritical of me to accuse you of reducing a relationship to a happy meme because I enjoyed taking photos of what we did together. But I never gave a shit if our hashtag game was strong or if it looked like we were projecting this illusion of being a perfect couple. I just wanted to show you off, you asshole.

I wanted my friends to know that I was happy if even for a minute with someone who I thought was a genuinely nice guy.

Maybe I'm reaching too deep into trying to assume you have some actual depth, but maybe you hate pictures because you can't stand to actually see yourself as you are. A scared, immature little shit who thinks the whole world's against him.

I understand that it may be weird that I'm still good friends with an ex. I get that it makes you a little jealous even. And I get why. Your ex was a huge bitch and I'm sorry she cheated on you, and that you had to see a video of it online. But Jesus, you never shut the fuck up about her.

Anything I do wrong immediately makes you compare me to her. We are both females who were attracted to you. That's about where the similarities end. I'm not her and none of the mistakes I made should reflect her. It's a completely unfair thing to say.

I get it. You've been hurt. Like a lot. But grow up and move the fuck on. That's not all there can be in your life. I never told you this, but that's the reason I noticed you at that party. You were going on to someone about that stupid girl from that summer camp up in Palo Alto. She broke your heart in a fucked up way and I'm sorry. But you aren't the only one that's ever happened to. This pain doesn't belong to you and neither do they.

Maybe you just shut down after that. The guy you describe in that story had a lot more guts than the guy I've known for 4 months. He sure as hell respected women a lot more.

You're probably trying to list off all the things you did or bought for me that you think I should be grateful for. Maybe even making a tally of all the times I never said thank you or appeared unimpressed. And that's honestly because I was. I didn't want big expensive parties in loft houses to show me that you were someone I should be with. Maybe your ex did. But I didn't. I just wanted to spend time with you and for you to not be leaving your thoughts at the office or on whatever secret porn project you were working on.

I just wanted you to be all in with me today and every yesterday before.

Not Back There.

That's not the way I want to live. Which is why I can't get sagged down with you anymore.

I don't know if you'll ever know what it's like to be in love with someone who processes emotions like a conspiracy theory waiting to be debunked or proven right. I don't think I ever said that I loved you in person because I couldn't handle the shattering silence of your stunted reaction. I mean, can you even comprehend what it would have meant for me to say that to you? Would it have made any difference to you? Or would you have just lied to me and told me what I wanted to hear?

I guess I'm sorry for a lot of things, too. Maybe I started too many fights with you unnecessarily. And probably over stupid things (it wasn't your fault your ex kept trying to get into contact with you even after you blocked her on literally everything). And I'm sorry I couldn't be stronger and do more to point this out to you when I could have actually helped you.

I'm sorry that we can't be friends. I'd love to be in your life in some capacity. But I understand you probably aren't ready for that if you still have my phone number blocked. Mostly I wish everything I'm saying doesn't fill you with even more spite. I don't think you can handle that.

I wish you nothing but the best.

Love,

J_____

P.S. Good call on Ted Cruz dropping out before the convention. I wanted to believe he'd stay in and make Trump's life a living hell but it looks like we'll be stuck with him and hopefully Bernie for the general election. I'm really gonna miss watching the election coverage with you.

I owe you a drink if I ever see you again.

PHANTOM OF THE H.S.A.M

They call it a residency to narrow down the parameters of what the hell it is. It's more of a treehouse without the trunk to garble it together. It's in fact the outside set of stairs and adjoining stairwells of the building next to it.

No space is left unnoticed or uncovered. Cardboard, squishy bubble wrap, and ropes dangle from every section. They are laid down in clumps of twelve so as to create support for the base. Roadblocks are reframed as doorways. Yellow legal pad paper covers discarded unassembled Ikea furniture. Blue tape tethers the loose ends. Gold spray paint hastily mashes into pink and purple to form something mistaken for a canvas. Sheetrock forms the illusion of beanbags. Castles of books with DVDs as moats line one section. A sole screen on a revolving table. It plays a Kevin Costner film endlessly to remind you that the world ended. This is the exception to the rule of "nothing intangible." A set of flickering light bulbs dangle from a rope at the top of the catacombs. Cutouts of Bonnie and Clyde and Mickey and Mallory on the first level. The pine from fallen oaks hug the shadows cast by the Christmas lights.

All throughout, Words: Revolution, Surrender, Selflessness, Unrequitable, Fireball, Effervescent. Words with disparate connections tied together by fishing lining.

There are layers upon worlds here. Caverns with seemingly no depths. Structures with the absence of hierarchy. Insularity as a myth that was left out of the oral tradition.

It is a reckless shelter for these apocalyptic days. Amplifying the Bad and Minimal Good. All are welcome. But no one is ever properly invited.

The building which my secret universe of stairwells is stapled to moonlights as both a club and a theater. My penance for my shortsightedness in the General-All-Of-It is to operate as the venue's eternal AV technician.

And, of course, you're starring in a production here.

For months I man the scaffolds, tiptoeing with the deliberateness of a prisoner trying to escape his captors. I cast the lights your way, setting the course for the future broken boys who will lament for that exact moment when they first saw your face. Your outfits change and embolden with the seasonal tilts. Your expressions retain the bronze steel of their jaw-dropping sincerity through all the whipped cream and sunscreen applied to your skin per setup. Your movements always a step closer to the other side of spontaneity.

This ritual persists for a time that even Bill Murray would consider obscene.

On other nights when you aren't there, when the afterlife of the theater/commune/nightclub is pulled into the strobe lights, I slip my way into the fortress.

A whiskey sour, a foreigner, and a Molly capsule are ingredients for the ceaseless glory always out of grasp.

On the night in question, a slew of monitors descends into the theater company interrupting the dress rehearsal.

Armando Christian Pérez (Pitbull) has won the Democratic Primary. He is now poised to run against Abby Huntsman in the 2032 Presidential Election.

I am standing on the far end watching the spectacle unfold. Pitbull's song with Keisha comes on leading to a spontaneous dance party.

You turn around and lock eyes with me momentarily, and I attempt to evaporate into myself where I cannot be seen.

It's raining.

You follow.

From rope to rope, I leap to upper levels. You're running as quickly as you can.

You stop.

Someone is calling your name.

I descend to see where the tracks paused. He stands, holding your arms, and places a kiss on your cheek.

You embrace him and rest your head on his chest.

It's still raining.

He can't see me.

For some reason, he stamps out a cigarette and tells you frankly how to properly put one out so as to not light fire to the structure.

He is saying all of this in a British accent.

As his ginger hair casts a thick hue through the downpour, I see—magnified through the glimmer of black mirrored surveillance tapes—how inconsequential I actually am.

I make my way upstairs, him behind you still chatting away, you grasping at my leg.

I shake you loose and pause in one of the hardly stable constructed rooms.

"You promised the other was the last one," you say.

I fling my cape over my back dramatically and lower the visor of my Daft Punk-esque helmet.

Moving from scaffoldings, someone down below points in my direction and gasps, "Phantasmal!"

You say something about moving somewhere else, but I don't catch what.

A well-dressed Italian man carrying a statue of Jesus tears down the banners with the strung up words.

A German Artist Collective passes through moments after, wheatpasting the walls in faded brown with a phrase: *Know Hope.*

A short Irishman follows not long after that, and with his guitar, smashes the letters K & W into charcoal bits

Untitled Ben Howard/Frank Ocean Collaboration

[Verse 1] (Her)
Oh hey, I wasn't looking
I was listening to the primary in the sunshine state
And you, you'd slipped through the backdoor
Escaping into the cold climate-changed June

All of me gathers in motion
To watch the show that followed my own
Across Russian River summers held at maximum
Where independence leads to a thaw

[Bridge 1]
And now he's caught between
Slipping time a watch
And cautioning for green, green AstroTurf
Where commitment is meant to be nourished

[Chorus]
She's swimming in the metadata tonight
Swimming in metadata tonight
Yeah, swimming in metadata tonight
Swimming in metadata tonight
Swimming in metadata tonight
Swimming, yeah
Swimming in metadata tonight

[Verse 2] (Him)
Big spotlights shining on a charcoal stage
Look up to your girl, let's call her Everything
Everything
Watch her slip a nightgown off
Watch her hit her mark on a punchline
Everything
Watch her apply whipped cream to her smile
Watch her fix her thong
Watching the futuristic boys watch her fix her thong

[Bridge 2]

You're leaving the act at work
Bathing in neon discotheques
Wet and warned of using your phone
Flickering summer in every gesture
And now I don't know how to be there when I'm not
How to be there when I'm not

[Chorus]
He's swimming in the metadata tonight
Swimming in metadata tonight
Yeah, swimming in metadata tonight
Swimming in metadata tonight
Swimming in metadata tonight
Swimming, yeah
Swimming in metadata tonight

[Verse 3] (Me)
And you're the one
The ghost story rapping the song of two lovers in dissonance
The man in the middle between the digital lamp throwing and
shading
Misappropriating moments
Making synonyms of intimacy of surveillance
While holding clichéd hashtags ransom
Until they don't know if it's love or sousveillance

[Bridge 3]
And only I can see
That this is fidelity
Corrupted by insecurity
From a lack of empathy

Only I can see
Only I
Can see
See
Sea

DISPATCHES FROM THE CONVENTION FLOOR

You've been dreaming of an Electric Fuhrer.

And you're swearing, swearing it's a soundstage. Just a soundstage.

The uninsured extra playing a Ted Cruz delegate is dipping his head back for the eyedrops.

Someone will screw it up. It'll be a quick tilt pan and the porn star version of Mike Pence will knock over the green screen.

The convention floor is sliding gracelessly with flags toppling.

You're witnessing a ground plan for another World War.

"We don't want them in our country!" he says to applause.

You're swearing it can't happen here. That dark age that was predicted, neglected, and abandoned by the men huddling under a table in the West Wing with a tape recorder containing an 18-minute gap inside of it.

That's somewhere else's problem.

A wave of Time washes over you like an injection.

Women's Fitness magazines have been subsidized by the government. Chris Christie and Newt Gingrich alternate as cover stars to provide the women of America tips for how to slim down.

The sixteenth season of *The Apprentice* begins airing in September 2017. While constitutional scholars bicker over the legality of this unprecedented scenario, staffers and Democratic congressmen are routinely mistreated by the President on a weekly basis.

Breitbart News is given a $1.5 billion stimulus package and nationalized as a syndicated radio-streaming-VR service. They quickly buy out Fox News and commence rebranding.

Then, you're in Orlando a year later and a state of emergency is being called.

He's fulfilling the promise Ivanka made that he would be color-blind and gender-neutral.

A speech on that week's episode of *The Apprentice* ends up being the defining moment when inclusivity is co-opted.

After this speech, no one will ever again feel comfortable uttering the phrase LGBTQ.

The Advocate and other leading queer publications will remove the acronym from their letterheads. An editorial that varies in each will explain that the phrase has been tainted and in "this new America, alternate methods must be found to express identity and diversity."

Time rolls back again and indistinct chants of locking someone up are heard.

"*Critics* and *Cynics!*" the rest are called.

That's for anyone who stands in the way of their White Optimism.

"Law and Order!"

You swear you can see Chris Meloni squinting somewhere in the crowd.

"We'll get them all out. Criminal Aliens! Criminal Aliens!"

Will Smith and Tommy Lee Jones should be put on the case.

"All of them. We'll round 'em up. Humanely like real people, though. But then we'll get them the hell out of here!"

"And China! CHINA too!"

Then, he says he hears your voice. He says it after a while, though.

As if to remind you that he should at least try to finish you off after demanding you be on your knees for the pretty picture that it would make.

Did he think he'd ever see this?

Maybe that one time in a coke-filled rum den somewhere off Lower Chelsea back in the 90s.

There's this Soprano glide when he talks about police. Like they're his caporegime. To enforce a vision of injustice with no sympathy.

Is this happening here? Are you actually reading this, hearing this, seeing this and is it actually something that had to be written because it's happening *here*?

She's dreaming of a redundant nightmare that folded downwards when she reaches for the can of soda labeled DEMOCRACY with something illegible crossed out above it.

Are we going to double backwards because "Damn, dude, do you remember when that *ALMOST* happened?" is going be something repeated for generations every summer when they're stoned on their stoops listening to Frank Ocean's fifth and sixth and they'll get it, the way Germany finally did? Is that the best example you can come up with?

"On January 20th of 2017," he says to a laugh in a quiet room. "The American people will finally wake up to a country where the laws of the United States are enforced!"

Is he plagiarizing the show? Or the Stallone Dredd film? Or both?

"These are the facts plainly and honestly. We honor the American people with the truth and nothing else. So sorry Lies! We don't have time to be Politically Correct!"

And then the man from Chicago hears his legacy by namesake— threatened to be torn apart.

He paces his study between the 4-6 hours he allots for sleep and considers the state he has built in the form of a Kienholz brand car with five studs.

He considers the insult perhaps most misdirected at him during his time in office.

MUSLIM.

How it is meant as a slur. And how that slur under a smaller set of thumbs is a template for voyeurism's big brother.

The engine's running on the black Kienholz. The key has been inserted. It waits for the gloaming. For a turn.

Time oozes like a confession and you've arrived at the first day of Tomorrow.

The founder of the Oculus Rift presents in a massive televised conference a VR presentation of America under a jihadist takeover.

Bill O'Reilly describes it as an "unnerving call to take immediate action."

The 115th Congress rushes ahead a bill titled the "Law Through Liberty Act" which delicately removes the language of the 4th amendment as it applies to mosques.

The law is immediately challenged by the ACLU and NAACP and brought before the Supreme Court.

With Peter Thiel having been appointed as the ninth justice, Law Through Liberty is upheld.

The Draconian tech company that Thiel cofounded, Palantir, is given free rein to begin routine inspections of mosques involved in alleged terrorist plots.

Which according to the standards set by Law Through Liberty, is all of them.

An absolute Wall that is a stand-in for the administration's legacy is expensively erected not long after.

Panopticon-brand drone satellites glide over El Paso and San Diego.

The anti-war patriots retreat further into an underground that will later be hearkened to as "the new 50s."

Sean Hannity's erection will rip through the seams of his pants when he declares, "That was his best speech yet!" for the 7th time that year.

WikiLeaks begins singling out specific cable news hosts for subsequent humiliation.

A video of a drunk Eric Bolling liberally dropping the n-word as he listens to the new Kendrick Lamar album is released.

Greg Gutfield, who once called for all of the secrets of Assange's people to be released so they would know how it felt, is shown to have been a large donor to Scientology.

Counterattacks in the form of DDOs hacks which trace back to Russian IP addresses cripple the WikiLeaks network.

A FISA court ruling gives the intelligence community reign to target offshore data havens both "physical and ephemeral in order to target enemies of the state."

3 months into his presidency and somewhere in between a friendly golf match with Putin, the extradition of Snowden is discussed.

Edward Snowden is brought back for a speedy trial that is not open to the public and is quickly sentenced to death by gas chamber for treason.

Devices for #bragging will become kaleidoscopes for the 53rd state, the NSA.

Every unpaid intern will gawk at the snaps you carelessly shuttle back and forth.

Rebels will resume communication via owls; old forms of romance will embolden.

Such details are what will be on the secret menu version of El Boss' speeches, right next to Animal Style Fries.

Jake Tapper, while still in exile in Chile, will publish at age 67, *American Frankenstein,* what many historians will call the essential text of the Trumpian era.

It will be viewed alongside such classics as *All the President's Men* and *Fear and Loathing on the Campaign Trail* as an essential document of its political times.

It will implicate a vast swath of media figureheads from his own network in particular. A key component will document the independent research he began regarding the rise of the alt-right. This will be the definitive look into its evolution from a group of fringe white chauvinists to tech company CEOs.

Evidence provided will serve in the senate hearings regarding the process by which these social media platforms and sites were transformed into massive satellites for the surveillance state to locate political and PC enemies, thus initiating the Great Purge of 2019.

Various anchors on Fox News will be compared to Neville Chamberlain. Those comparisons will, in retrospect, appear too harsh for Chamberlain and too light for the likes of Glenn Beck, Bill O'Reilly and Megyn Kelly.

John Oliver's assassination will be viewed as the equivalent of a JFK moment.

Anderson Cooper's execution in the Giants Stadium in San

Francisco alongside his longtime lover will be seen as the era's RFK moment.

And Jon Stewart's subsequent car bombing on the verge of his HBO show's miraculously renewed second season will be seen as its MLK.

Images of millennial tears collect quietly in the last Latino bar in the city when time builds itself painfully around you and you're driving through a tunnel in Half Moon Bay.

You're passing that loner beach where sunsets skip hopscotch memories of a summer camp that is already gone.

You stand in the ruins where you first met Her without memories or plans as another crescendo of Time fills you.

It's October 7th, 2016. Julian Assange has brought his life's work full circle with a promise delivered.

Building off the leaked DNC emails which unseated Debbie Wasserman Schultz as the chair of the Democratic National Committee days before the convention, he unleashes a set of transcripts from Hillary Clinton's speeches to various financial institutions including Goldman Sachs.

On this same day audio is leaked from a conversation with Billy Bush from *Access Hollywood* revealing Donald Trump saying, "When you're a star, they let you do it. You can do anything ... Grab them by the pussy. You can do anything,"

The debate on October 9th in St. Louis is the most watched debate in history. That afternoon, Trump manages to clobber Hillary into a 20 second silence that she cannot recover from.

Clinton's poll numbers sink. Surrogates (especially celebrities) struggle to rationalize the rhetoric. Too many reveal themselves as 1% opportunists in the process and are subsequently devalued. Somehow Trump's misogynistic comments regarding his ability to casually sexually assault women do nothing to destroy his presidential campaign.

This is the point on the darkest timeline that you have been sent back to intervene at.

Time casts you back one last time in a convertible on PCH driving towards a paper background sunset with compost all around.

There's disaster porn everywhere but at long last you've arrived outside of yourself.

And this is what you do next.

PROPOSAL FOR
AN EMPATHETIC
SURVEILLANCE STATE

Project Statement: The plausibility of a Trump presidency has alarmed America for an endless number of reasons. Chief amongst them is the idea that he is a soft dictator who would abuse the powers of the executive branch in order to settle political scores and benefit himself. The method by which he would go about achieving many of his proposed policy aims is mass surveillance.

Should a Trump presidency become a reality, the Orwellian apparatus that is the NSA would be at his absolute disposal. Policies such as the mass deportation of millions of Latino immigrants and the rooting out of homegrown radical Islamic terrorists could only be achieved through the implementation of a massive surveillance system to target these individuals. And there is no guarantee that they would be entirely effective. As is the case with so many of these broad policies (e.g. Stop and Frisk) individuals would be unfairly singled out. This does not even take into account the likelihood of these devices being turned on to Trump's many political enemies, including journalists.

Background & Historical Context: Following the recent release of incriminating transcripts featuring Hillary Clinton praising the financial sector and in incredibly transparent terms promising "to manage the status quo," Republican presidential candidate Donald Trump has surged in the polls. Indisputable statements such as these play perfectly into the narrative of the Trump campaign of a broken system which favors only the established elite in Washington.

And while these statements objectively reveal a candidate whose only true constituency is The Establishment, the manner and motives by which they were revealed is incredibly problematic. And not just to conflicted voters who must choose between either Godzilla or King Kong to rule their half-destroyed city. But to the project of Democracy itself.

Julian Assange's revelations are perfectly in line with the ideology that guides WikiLeaks: one of a world with perfect transparency. His view imagines a world where government corruption and wrongdoing is always second-guessed because of the existence of a WikiLeaks-like entity which might reveal such wrongdoing. It is intended to *force* a form of sincere transparency.

But Assange is wrong this time.

What Assange's approach has *always* failed to take into account is the collateral damage accrued through his revelations. He has boasted time and time again about published documents unedited without regard for redactions. This unwavering policy is what led his biggest media partners (*The New York Times* and *The Guardian*) to break ties with him following the Cablegate revelations of 2010. The unredacted versions he released implicated undercover sources who provided the necessary information that Assange would tout as making his organization the effective whistleblowing device of the twenty-first century.

This continued up until recently with the DNC hacks that I participated in which implicated a vast swath of individuals, many of whom lost their jobs and were publicly humiliated unnecessarily as a result. Subsequent bulk leaks around the time of the DNC hack (namely those pertaining to the attempted coup in Turkey) revealed medical records, the names of rape victims, and individuals in Saudi Arabia who privately identified as homosexual.

Let me state for the record, I don't feel any remorse for what we released. The corruption inherent within the Democratic Party needed to be exposed. But after seeing the lack of remorse on behalf of WikiLeaks for the "little people" who are swept up into the broader leaking schemes, it's dawned on me that this approach is not one that is ethical in spite of how Assange and his associates may try to rationalize it. The collateral damages in this particular scenario of the election are, for better or worse, the American people.

With all of this in mind, it has occurred to me that the approach of radical transparency without redactions and without sympathy for those whom it may indirectly influence needs an urgent update.

Artist's statement: My practice has revolved around sullying the lines between transparency and the self. I have targeted high-powered individuals as a means to reach those who are in their sphere of influence. Upon further review, I've realized this approach isn't very effective overall. Currently, my approach is to tap into the zeitgeist (in this case via a highly contentious presidential election) and parse out alternatives that would otherwise seem ripped from a dystopian novel in any other election year.

Past Works & Leaks

2016
"DNC Email Scandal," (in collaboration with Guccifer 2.0), Philadelphia, PA

"Third Anthony Weiner Sexting Scandal," New York, New York.

"Melania & Ivanka Trump Nudes," (unreleased)

"The Trump Card Scandals," (forthcoming)

2015
"Amateur Rapper Gives It to Amateur Muse Sex Tape," Atlanta, GA

2014
"New Year's Day Release of S_____ From 4.6 million Accounts," Venice, CA

"iCloud Celebrity Hacking Scandal aka Celebgate aka The Fappening," Venice, CA/Chicago, IL/Lancaster, PA

2009
"Jenny Horner Conversations with Eric Bloshfield," Jeffersonville, IN

Project Intent: Recent dystopian fictional narratives, such as *Mr. Robot,* provide a vision of a very possible present in light of a hacker revolution, it's dawned on me that alternatives are needed. Such fictional scenarios refuse to show the world that is intended to replace the world that is being critiqued. I do not intend to plunge our world into absolute chaos without at least a schematic for a way out of it, à la *Mr. Robot.* Therefore, I intend to show that another world is in fact possible.

Budget: Whatever it is that the NSA is allotted for federally (an undisclosed and unreliable amount) but let's imagine about 1/3 of that considering how much consolidating we'll be doing.

STEPS TOWARD AN EMPATHETIC SURVEILLANCE STATE

Part 1: The Crash

We begin with the biggest social media leak of all time. This will be executed through an old fashioned cryptography hack called a man-in-the-middle attack. This involves a hacker secretly intercepting and relaying messages between two parties that believe they are directly communicating with one another. Typically, this is a means of simply intercepting information as was the case when the NSA was revealed to have experimented with impersonating Google in order to begin bulk-collecting data from citizens.

The key difference in my man-in-the-middle attack is that I will not be a passive observer.

This will be a gargantuan, geo-targeted attack singling out male users of S_____.

It is the kind of attack that only a privileged insider like myself would be able to execute. There will be digital fingerprints all across the decrypted servers that I crash that will not be able to be erased. The FBI will begin their manhunt almost immediately and the trail will lead directly to me.

In the meantime, the company will be left in shambles. Countless users' information is exposed in a humiliating manner. No male celebrity or public figure with a S_____ account is left unscathed as a result. All will have something to reveal. From a secret fetish to a secret crush to a secret lover. All are leveled down to a mass tree stump of embarrassing fashion.

The company having just gone public days before sees its stock plummet quickly and drastically, thus beginning the implosion of the Tech Bubble.

Part 2: Gore & Wreckage

Following the *Tech Crash of 2016*, senators and pundits scramble for answers. Most are proposed under a guise of a variation of the phrase "We never saw it coming." Leaks in subsequent days prove this cannot possibly be true.

Considering the wide dragnet of S_____ accounts exposed via this grandiose leak (aka all North American males) it is unsurprising that incriminating information regarding Donald Trump is released. The actual specifics of this currently remain unclear but they could be any combination of things. Is it someone bragging about Trump's business ties with Russia? A lawyer ogling at a stripper while he candidly proclaims how he and Trump are getting away with paying NO taxes *again* for another year? A snap of Trump snorting cocaine off a melquiladora's ass while sipping Mezcal with El Chapo?

It ultimately doesn't matter because one, or all, of these revelations begin the rational transparent downfall of the most openly fascist American presidential candidate of all time.

Part 3: The Junkyard

Below are the necessary and rational steps needed to reform the surveillance state following the crash.

Severing the Slick Black Cord: The Supreme Court must begin hearing a lawsuit brought against the tech companies in the wake of *The Tech Crash of 2016*. The point of this is to at least *consider* the legality of the tricky relationship between all the massive tech companies and their relationship to the NSA and other security intelligence groups.

Break the Big Data Cartel: Immediately halt every major surveillance program revealed by Edward Snowden (this includes but is not limited to: PRISM, XKeyscore, SIGINT, etc.). They will most likely resume under some legal maneuvering but in their hiatus, all NSA technicians, operators, engineers and agents must undergo a mandatory ethical training (such as the one alluded to in this proposal) or they will be removed from their position.

Drag the Law into the Light: Every FISA (Foreign Intelligence Surveillance) court session and ruling must be livestreamed publicly at a reasonable hour.

A New Amendment: The twenty-eighth (as of yet unnamed) amendment to the Constitution will be introduced to Congress in order to be ratified by every state. It will extend the provisions of the fourth amendment in regards to prohibiting unlawful searches and seizures to the digital domestic space of the Internet. Warrants issued by judges such as those serving on the FISA court will also have to provide warrants in order for ANY form of surveillance to begin on an individual's private online space. This would set an, as of yet, unestablished precedent: a constitutionally legal acknowledgment of the Internet's role in our lives.

The Media Bill of Rights: None of these proposed alterations will mean anything unless a functioning fourth estate is present to inform the public about these changes. Don't want angry and out of control alternative news outlets such as WikiLeaks to exist? Then fix and/or replace the damn problem. And do so legally in a way that makes the insane standards of today's media realm nonexistent. The first step would be a stimulus package for distressed newspaper outlets in cities all across the country. It will come with a kind of contract that this money can only be accepted under the condition that the paper properly be managed and free from standards regarding to complying with advertisers or investors. Newspapers would essentially be untouched and widely distributed forms free of a *bottom line* much like NPR or Democracy Now!

The details as they pertain to cable news will have to be different considering the complexities of that world with which I am not familiar. Instead I nominate that Tom Brokaw, Jon Stewart, Amy Goodman, Joy Reid and Jorge Ramos write the set of regulations and ethics that all cable news networks must now begin adhering to.

Shutting Down the Utah Data Center: Construction on the massive data archive by the NSA in Utah must end. It is a massive waste of taxpayer money and is expected to use 1.7 million gallons of water per day in order to operate. A law (the 4th Amendment Protection Act) will be proposed by the group Nullify NSA and must be adopted by the Utah legislature. It would ban all state and local agencies from providing tangible support to the NSA as long as it continues its mass surveillance programs. Cutting off their water supply, their key resource, would effectively end the data center.

Another law will be passed to make the remains of the Utah Data Center into a state-recognized piece of land art.

Architecture of Transparency: The NSA building must replace its black stain glass windows with a transparent set. Public tours of every section must be readily available and led by skilled docents.

Pardons: Presidential pardons must be issued immediately to Edward Snowden, Chelsea Manning, and any whistleblowers from the past 10 years, specifically those targeted by the Obama Administration.

Part 4: New Models Today

The world we may wake up in tomorrow will no longer resemble its form only hours ago. And should the dust of the ensuing chaos of all these events settle we would still all be involved in a deeply troubling relationship with the tools of mass surveillance. Namely our phones. And Facebook. And Instagram. And everything that allows the freedom to look through postmodern windows into a life that is not your own. All of these things would still exist. We would still *want* to be seen. And *want* to see others as well.

So if this is what we are stuck with for the time being, this is what I propose:

Instead of looking at events with envy or suspicion, recast that eye with empathy. Don't look at the woman with a hijab as a potential co-conspirator to the man with ties to ISIS who committed a horrible crime.

See her as a grieving mother who is as shocked as any of the families of the victims. See her as she struggles to understand why her son would do this. How she might struggle with the guilt that somehow this is indirectly her fault. See her try to find comfort in her religion for which she is being unfairly targeted. See her as a mother in pain.

Take all the plot threads around envy and comparisons and imagine them as doorways into teleport shuttles.

Transfer yourself entirely into other narratives. Ask yourself questions about them. Consider *why* they feel a certain way and why that makes them post x or y. Consider it from a distanced approach. And don't consider your own feelings in the process. These stories are not yours and they never can be.

Reconstruct your vision. Undo the perspective you have of viewing lovers as potential terrorists.

Consider the Probable: the world rotates without you. Your ex might actually be happy at this very moment that you are looking at them. The other person might be the right fit for them in a way you never were or could be. And they may not have been the right person for *you* all along.

Look at those moments that they are trying to project of their happiness. Don't insert yourself into that photograph. It wasn't meant for you. Your happiness is elsewhere. Theirs exists right in front of you and if you ever did love or care for this person it should mean everything to you that they have found a molecule of happiness with someone else.

Share *that* with them.

See all these differences, all these flaws and keep that sense of awe. Every feeling and hope of every person on the planet is bigger than the metadata file you can compress them into.

Do this. Every day. Embrace the short fiction stories in your newsfeed every day. Realize this method may be here to stay. Realize this future you've all collectively embraced may not get an amendment or reform anytime soon. Realize the peace from seeing them all as they are. Realize change begins when you call it even if it's a promise you can't always keep. Realize your pain must be embraced in order to be released. Realize it so you can assist others release theirs. Realize this now. Realize it now because this is the only now you get.

Biography

C_____ was born and raised in Jeffersonville, Indiana (making him the second person of Hispanic heritage from Indiana to be relevant this election cycle). He enjoys hiking, taking photos, and other various private activities. He hopes to be exonerated and return to his apartment in Venice, California someday. He currently resides in an undisclosed location in Argentina.